THE MIDNIGHT LIBRARY

Blood and Sand

LOOKING FOR DAYLIGHT? KEEP DREAMING.

THE MIDNIGHT LIBRARY CONTINUES. . . .

VOICES

BLOOD AND SAND

END GAME

THE CAT LADY

THE MIDNIGHT LIBRARY

Blood and Sand

Damien Graves

SCHOLASTIC INC.
New York Toronto London Auckland Sydney
Mexico City New Delhi Hong Kong Buenos Aires

SPECIAL THANKS TO DAVID SAVAGE

—

ISBN 0-439-87187-5

Series created by Working Partners Ltd.

12 11 10 9 8 7 6 5 4 3 2 1 6 7 8 9 10 11/0

Printed in the U.S.A.
First printing, September 2006

Welcome, reader.

My name is Damien Graves,
curator of that secret
institution:

The Midnight Library.

Where is The Midnight Library, you ask?
Why have you never heard of it?
For the sake of your own safety, these questions are better left
unanswered. However . . . as long as you promise not to reveal
where you heard the following (no matter who or *what*
demands it of you), I will reveal what I
keep here in my ancient vaults.
After many years of searching,
I have gathered the most terrifying
collection of stories known to
humanity. They will chill you to
your very core, and make
the flesh creep on your young,
brittle bones. So go ahead, brave
soul. Turn the page. After all, what's
the worst that could happen . . . ?

Damien Graves

THE MIDNIGHT LIBRARY: VOLUME II

Stories by David Savage

CONTENTS

Blood and Sand

"Bored! Bored! Bored!" yelled John, drowning out the roar of the waves washing onto the shore, and the shrieking seagulls overhead.

Sarah didn't really blame her brother for not being in much of a vacation spirit. The sky was gray, and the sea didn't look remotely inviting. It looked cold, dangerous, and mean, its foamy waves daring them to come closer. An icy wind rolled along the beach, lifting up the coarse sand and flinging it in their faces. It felt sharp, like it was trying to carve slices out of them.

Even without the wind, it was hardly the most pleasant of beaches to stroll along, anyway. The sand was strewn with litter, and it smelled a bit weird, too. The rocks farther down the beach were covered in some kind of gooey green sea-slime. And beyond the rocks was the broken and boarded-up pier, long closed down. It stood there, jutting out over the grayish waters, its cast-iron girders turning rusty and covered in seaweed.

All in all, John and Sarah would have preferred to be in a nice, sunny resort, ideally somewhere far away — with a big swimming pool and a beautiful sandy beach next to a warm blue ocean.

Trying to take her brother's mind off his misery, Sarah picked up a shell. "Listen, you really *can* hear the sea," she said, holding it to her ear.

"You don't *need* to put a shell against your ear to hear the sea around here," John said pointedly. "You're right *next* to it!" He bent down and picked up a pebble, then faced the water and flicked his wrist. The pebble was supposed to skim horizontally across the surface, leaping and bounding as it went, but it just sank. "Even the stones don't skim right," he said in disgust.

Sarah thought it wasn't really fair to blame the stone, but she knew it was better not to argue with her brother when he was in a bad mood. And right now he was in a *very* bad mood. John had grown to hate the seaside resort more and more each year. If Sarah was honest with herself, so had she. And now, here they were again, bored stiff already, and it was only the second day of their vacation.

John was thirteen now and Sarah twelve, and they'd been coming here since they were toddlers. There were the photos to prove it. Shots of them both trudging around on the sand in their diapers. They looked like they'd enjoyed these vacations way back then, but not anymore. Yet whenever they complained, Mom would exclaim, "But coming here has become a family tradition! And one day, maybe you'll bring your own children here, as well."

"As a punishment, you mean?" John would reply sarcastically.

But Mom would just ignore him. She refused to hear anything bad said about the resort, completely failing to realize that there was absolutely nothing for John and Sarah to do here.

Sarah looked down the beach at the pier. It looked like a huge piece of debris that had been washed in by the tide and left to rot. She and John both remembered, though only just, when it had been fully functioning, filled with rides and arcades, and its own fortune-teller.

Everything else interesting in the small town seemed to have closed down, too. There were no movies any-more — the two theaters were both boarded up now. The annual fair had moved to the next town. There was no aquarium, no miniature golf anymore, either.

There was one small arcade left, but the games were old and boring. The fast-food shops all served food so sodden with grease that even John, who loved junk food, refused to eat it. Mostly they sold stale-smelling burgers and fried chicken. There was one pizza parlor where the food was at least edible. But even Mom complained that the sauce was watery and the cheese a little rubbery.

Sarah sighed. "There must be *something* we can do," she said.

She hesitated, then added, "How about we enter the sand-sculpting competition again?" She looked over at the section of beach alongside the promenade that had been fenced off for the resort's one remaining big annual event. Entrants would mold and carve wet sand, like clay, into shapes and structures, and then paint it. The most impressive creation would win a cash prize. She and John had entered the competition the year before — it had been the first year they'd been old enough to. And though they had been the youngest competitors, they'd done really well and had come in second. But John had sulked for the best part of a week because they hadn't won. Sarah had just enjoyed taking part, but she knew how competitive her brother could be.

"No point," snapped John. "The Sandman's bound to win. And it's no fun when you know you'll lose." He flicked another stone at the sea. "No fun at all."

When that stone also sank without a single skim, he turned and began to trudge along the beach again. "Why can't there be just one year when the Sandman doesn't enter?" he asked. "Just one!" He scuffed the ground with his foot. "Why can't he just stay away and let someone else win for a change? It isn't fair."

Sarah followed, thinking about the Sandman. His real name was Gavin Bronson, but everyone referred to him as the Sandman. He was some weird old guy who lived locally and happened to be great at sand sculpting. His sculptures were amazingly realistic, and he'd won the competition every year since anyone could remember — always seeming to surpass what he'd done the year before.

Sarah thought back to the Sandman's previous entries. The first one she could remember clearly was a huge arrangement of fruit. Everything — the bananas, the bunches of grapes, even the pineapple — had looked perfect. One of Sarah's favorites had been a very life-like donkey, so realistic you were almost tempted to go over and feed it carrots.

"What did he win with last year?" asked John.

"Clunkers," Sarah replied.

"Oh, yeah — Clunkers," John echoed.

"We haven't seen old Clunkers so far this year, have we?" Sarah observed with surprise. "That's strange — he's always here." Clunkers was an old dog that seemed to live on the beach, pawing the sand and sniffing around for food, or squatting in the shade of the promenade wall on the rare occasions that the sun came out. Last year, the Sandman had done an incredibly lifelike sculpture of Clunkers, staring out to sea. It had, of course, been the winning entry.

"Maybe the fame of having his sand sculpture win the competition went to Clunkers' head, and he left the resort for a better one," John suggested with a grin.

Sarah laughed. "Why don't we enter again anyway?" she said to her brother. "Just for the fun of it — just to keep busy."

John shrugged. "I'll think about it," he said.

They were near the rotting, abandoned pier now. The beach all around it was fenced off, too, forbidden to both tourists and locals all year-round. Signs were propped up along the fence, telling everyone to keep out — not that you'd have wanted to enter anyway. Even the seagulls seemed to keep away from the area.

Through the gaps in the fence, Sarah could see that the shadowed sand beneath the pier looked more like dirt, and was covered in rotting seaweed and debris that had been washed up by the tides. "That pier looks haunted to me," she said.

"And so does that house next to it," John added, pointing to a ramshackle old bungalow that looked as run-down and uncared for as the pier it overlooked.

As they looked at the bungalow, a familiar figure

dressed in a stylish, light-colored jacket and pants came out through the front door, locking it behind him.

"It's *him*!" Sarah said. "The Sandman. That must be where he lives!"

"And I thought he'd live in some big sand castle somewhere!" said John, kidding around.

Sarah stared at the Sandman's finely boned face. It had an unnatural brown tinge, as if he had spent far too much time out in the sunshine. In contrast, his eyes were as black as the night sea. "He seems to get creepier every year. . . ." she said with a shiver.

John turned to watch the Sandman make his way down the promenade. "I bet he's off to work on his sand sculpture," he said, looking thoughtful. "Of course, it might be worth us entering if we had some idea of what we had to beat. . . ." he added.

Sarah stared at him. "Are you suggesting what I think you're suggesting?" she asked in surprise.

John nodded. "If we got to see what the Sandman is making for this year's competition," he said, "we could try to create something even better."

"But you know he always hides his sculptures in a special tent," Sarah said, "so nobody gets to see them before judging day." Then she smiled, putting on an innocent look. "But if someone were to sneak inside . . ."

John was looking much more cheerful now. "Exactly," he said. "Yeah, we *will* enter that competition. Whatever the Sandman makes, we'll top it. We just have to see what he's doing, then figure out how to go one better."

"That's the spirit!" Sarah laughed, imitating her mom's voice.

They turned and walked back to the fenced-off section of the beach where the sand-sculpting competition took place. They could see that a few people had already begun their entries. A large red-and-white–striped beach tent covered up one of the little plots of sand.

"That's got to be the Sandman's," said John.

They went to the entrance of the competition area and collected the entry forms. They were just in time — tomorrow was the closing date.

That evening, they filled in the forms and then asked their mom to sign her consent.

"That's the spirit!" she said, looking delighted. "You see! Where else could you have so much fun!"

Sarah and John grinned at each other. Their mom was so predictable.

The following morning, after turning in their forms, Sarah and John were shown to a plot of sand in the competition area.

"The Sandman's said he's doing a very special piece this year," a nearby entrant said to Sarah, noticing her and John staring at the Sandman's tent. "I wonder what it'll be!" Then he returned to his own sculpture, a larger-than-life chess set spread across the sand.

"Hopefully *we* won't be wondering what's in that tent for much longer," John muttered to Sarah under his breath.

"So you still want to go ahead with the plan?" Sarah asked him.

John nodded.

Sarah felt a pang of regret. Part of her wished that they could just enjoy the competition for the fun of it, like their neighbor. But John was so hung up on winning. "OK, so how'll we get in there without him catching us?" she asked.

"We'll just pretend to be experimenting with ideas

in the sand, but really we'll be watching and waiting," said John. "He has to leave that tent sometime."

Luckily, there was an ice-cream truck parked just outside the competition area, to keep them stocked up with provisions. John kept watch while Sarah brought over two cones, and then later, Sarah kept watch while John brought over two ice pops.

Finally, the Sandman, with his jacket draped over one arm, shirtsleeves rolled up, left his tent.

"I think he's heading for the restroom," said John.

"Better him than me," Sarah replied, making a face. Most of the restrooms at the beach were filthy and had been vandalized. There were hardly ever any toilet seats or working taps in them, let alone soap or towels, and they all stank. She hated having to use them.

John tugged her arm. "Come *on*, we don't have much time."

The other entrants were busy concentrating on their own sand sculptures as John and Sarah crept around to the side of the Sandman's tent where no one could see what they were doing.

Sarah held up the edge of the tent while John crawled under, then she followed him in.

In the shadowed light, the sculpture looked quite eerie and made Sarah feel all goose-bumpy. It was a big sea-life sculpture. She gazed at the totally realistic shapes of crabs, lobsters, fish, and starfish — there was even a small shark. And the centerpiece was an octopus. Like the other sculpted sea creatures, the octopus was amazingly realistic. All eight tentacles were so perfectly done, Sarah could truly imagine them pulling the octopus along the murky ocean floor. Each suction cup — and there were hundreds of them — had been perfectly shaped and molded down each of those long, rubbery arms.

The octopus sculpture was so lifelike that Sarah found herself mesmerized by it. Unable to resist, she reached forward to touch one of the tentacles. Still damp, the sand crumbled and fell away at her touch. Sarah gave a sharp intake of breath, dismayed at having damaged the sculpture. And then she sprang back in shock as she saw what the fallen sand had revealed underneath.

Real octopus flesh.

"John," she gasped. "Look at —"

"Shhh!" John interrupted.

Sarah saw he was listening to something outside the tent and listened, too.

"No, I never reveal what my sculpture is going to be. You'll have to wait and see," a well-spoken, dry-sounding voice was saying to someone outside.

It was the Sandman! He was on his way back to the tent!

John and Sarah scrambled back out the way they had entered. As Sarah pulled the striped canvas back down after her, she caught a glimpse of the Sandman's shoes walking into the tent's entrance on the other side.

"Whew! That was a close one!" said John, grinning, as they made their way back over to their own plot of sand.

"We didn't have time to cover our tracks," Sarah said worriedly. "We'll have left footprints in there!"

"Don't worry," John told her. "The Sandman might guess *someone* has been spying on his sculpture, but he won't know it was us. At least, I don't *think* he saw us."

"It's not just that he'll guess someone has seen his sculpture, John," Sarah said worriedly. "He'll also guess that now someone knows he's been cheating. . . ."

John stared at her. "What do you mean?" he asked.

Sarah told John what she had seen. She thought he'd be as horrified as her, but instead, he laughed.

"There *can't* have been a real octopus under the sand sculpture," he dismissed. "You're crazy."

"But I'm *sure* there was," Sarah insisted.

"So what are you saying?" John snapped, getting impatient now. "That the Sandman somehow dragged a real, live octopus out of the ocean and covered it in sand to pass it off as a sculpture?"

"Or stole it from an aquarium somewhere," Sarah argued. "Isn't there one in the next town?"

John shook his head. "I take back what I said before," he said, turning to examine the sand in their plot. "Now you sound *completely* crazy!"

Sarah stamped her foot in frustration. She knew what she'd seen. Then suddenly, Clunkers came into her mind. . . . "OK, so where's Clunkers, then?" she said hotly.

John stopped abruptly and turned back to face her. The noise of the waves crashed in the background. "What's that got to do with it?" he asked.

"Last year, the Sandman won with a sculpture of Clunkers, didn't he?" Sarah said. "And this year, Clunkers is nowhere to be seen. Maybe that's because the body of Clunkers was *inside* that winning sculpture. And what about the donkey sculpture a couple of years ago? Maybe there was a real donkey underneath that one!"

"Well . . . it *was* pretty realistic," John said. "But still . . ."

"And everyone knows that the Sandman's sculptures suddenly got better a few years ago," Sarah continued. "I remember Mom saying she remembers that when he first started entering the competition, his work wasn't very good at all. But suddenly, one summer, he began to do great stuff. Maybe he'd discovered that the best way to create realistic sculptures . . ."

". . . is by mounding sand around the real thing?" John finished.

"Yes!" Sarah replied, relieved that her brother now seemed to believe what she had seen.

"Let's get away from all this sand for a while," John said.

Sarah nodded. "OK — where do you want to go?" she asked.

"The Sandman's house," John replied. "If you're right, we might find some more evidence there. Let's go and peek through his windows. There's no danger while he's busy here in his tent."

The curtains at the front of the Sandman's run-down old bungalow were drawn.

"Let's look around the back," said John. "I bet if that creep does have anything to hide, he'd keep it at the back of his house, anyway. Nobody would ever see it there. Beyond the back garden, it's a sheer drop down to the beach."

"We don't want to be trapped if he turns up, though," Sarah said uneasily.

But John was already opening the rickety gate.

Sarah followed him. "We shouldn't be doing this," she said anxiously. "The Sandman could come back at any time." She leaned back against the fence, trying to keep a lookout down the promenade while John went to peer in through the back windows.

Sarah could see that the curtains weren't drawn, but the windows were smeared with grime. "Can you see anything?" she asked.

John's face pressed against the glass as he squinted

in. "It's hard," he said, "but from what I *can* see, it looks like a real mess in there."

"Just hurry up," Sarah said. Then suddenly, the section of fence she'd been leaning on, even more rotten than it looked, broke away and she was falling through the air.

She screamed, landing on the beach below with the wind knocked out of her. But at least she'd landed on soft, mushy sand and hadn't hurt herself.

"Sarah? Are you OK?" John called.

"I think so. . . ." Sarah called back. "Just a little shaken."

She put a hand down on the sand to push herself up, and felt something round and flat under her palm. She looked to see what it was.

Seconds later, John had made his way down to her. "What's that?" he asked curiously.

Sarah held up the little scratched, silvery disk. "It looks like an old coin or a medallion, or —" She stopped, an icy feeling grabbing at her throat, as she read the name on the disk. "See for yourself . . ." she said, holding it out to her brother.

"Looks like a dog tag," John said, positioning the metal disk to catch the light better so that he could read the inscription. "Clunkers . . ." he breathed. He looked down to where Sarah had found the tag. "Maybe Clunkers' remains are around here, too," he added.

Sarah shivered and pointed under the pier. "I bet the Sandman buried Clunkers there, where no one ever goes," she said.

"This is all condemned. The pier is meant to be demolished soon," John said, gazing around. "We'll get in trouble for sure if anyone sees us under here. Come on — let's get out of here."

John and Sarah got up and headed for where there was a gap in the fencing that surrounded the entire area.

"We should find out if the Sandman has buried Clunkers here," Sarah said to John as he pried the gap in the fence open so that she could climb through. "If he really is doing awful things, then someone needs proof to stop him."

John paused for a moment, and then sat down on the sand. Sarah sat down next to him. She could see that he was thinking seriously.

"If we go searching around in the daytime," John began slowly, "we'll get caught. So we'll come back tonight. We'll need a flashlight and a couple of shovels."

Sarah and John waited till after midnight, and then crept down the stairs of the small guesthouse where they were staying, armed with the two sturdy plastic shovels they'd bought from the one remaining beach store on the promenade. They went past the unattended reception desk, and out of the front door, quickly making their way down the dark street to the seafront. There was nobody around. After dark, the resort was like a ghost town.

The beach was abandoned, too, though the part with the sand-sculpture competition was still illuminated, giving the sand and seaweed an eerie, shimmering glow. Sarah quickly turned her gaze away. "Don't all the crabs come out onto the beach at night?" she said, trying to lighten the mood.

John pinched her side. "There's one now!" he laughed as he hurried down the stone steps to the sand.

Sarah hung back. Even the better part of the beach

looked creepy at this time of night, so she was dreading the closed-off forbidden part under the pier. The sea seemed glassy and mysterious, filled with the shapes of dangerous creatures. The swish of waves against the shore sounded like whispered warnings.

"Come on!" urged John.

Sarah took a deep breath and made her way down the steps, then they began to make their way along the sands to the dark shape that was the pier.

As they drew close, Sarah stopped in her tracks. It was *very* dark under there. The shadows looked as deep as the sea itself.

"Well, I don't see any signs telling us to keep out," John said, grinning.

Sarah knew he meant that the darkness had blotted out both the signs and their warnings. "We'll have to be careful," she cautioned. "There'll be all sorts of debris over there. Metal and glass and . . ."

"OK, OK!" John said in an exasperated tone. "You sound just like Mom!" He switched on his flashlight to look for a gap in the fenced-up area under the pier. The beam of light stopped on a board that was hanging loose. "Bingo!" John said.

He hurried over and squeezed through the gap, beckoning Sarah to do the same.

Reluctantly she did so — and immediately wrinkled her nose up. The smell of decaying seaweed was particularly strong from that side of the fence.

John cast the flashlight beam around under the pier.

No wonder it's so smelly, Sarah thought. She gazed at the masses of seaweed everywhere. It looked like an army of the stuff had slithered up the beach. She imagined it being full of jellyfish and eels, and thought about how terrible it would be to get your feet caught in it, and finally be swallowed up by it all.

"Amazing what gets washed up by the sea," John whispered. "I've always imagined all sorts of weird creatures live in the deep, and they all come out of the water at night — blubbery things with scales and tentacles, looking for people to drag back underwater with them. I bet they all hang around under the pier. They're probably waiting for us right now."

"Shut up, John. You don't scare me," Sarah lied. But she also began to worry that the Sandman might have seen them crossing the sand and would clamber down onto the beach to catch them. Or that he might be waiting until they were under the pier, in the deep dark, before pouncing on them.

"It's because of this thing that we have to come here every year, you know," said John.

"What do you mean?" Sarah asked, careful of where she placed her feet.

"Mom and Dad met under it," he replied. "Don't you remember them telling us? That's why this rotten town means so much to them, and why we're one of the last few families crazy enough to still visit the place."

"They met under *this* thing?" Sarah asked, surprised. "I must have forgotten!"

"It didn't used to be like this, though," John said. "Do you remember seeing Mom and Dad's old vacation photos from when they were young — before we were born? Back then, when the pier was open, it had shows and rides and a big Ferris wheel and a wax museum and stores and all kinds of games, and even a theater where comedians used to perform. And this part of the beach was open, too, and full of people on vacation. It was before the town got all run-down. They were both on vacation and met under here. Love at first sight, Mom said it was. He took her to one of the shows, and on some of the rides, and that's how they got together."

John pointed the flashlight upward, lighting the decaying hulk towering over their heads. It was hardly the most romantic place in the world these days.

"That's why Mom and Dad don't see the place as it is now," continued John. "They don't see the horrible sandwich shops, and the abandoned factories, and all the crumbling old buildings, and this" — he ran the flashlight beam across the pier's mighty girders — "dangerous, clapped-out heap of rusty old junk. They still see it as it was when they first met. And kid themselves that it's still a nice place and keep dragging us here, year after year after year!"

John picked up a big stone from the sand and hurled it at one of the steel beams. There was a great clang.

Sarah thought for a moment that the whole structure was going to collapse on top of them. "Do you want someone to catch us?" she said angrily. "Let's just start digging so we can get out of here."

"OK, sorry," said John.

They dug in silence for a little while.

"There's nothing here," said John, panting slightly. "Oh, wait — here's something! There seems to be something poking through the seaweed over here."

Sarah aimed the flashlight at it.

It was a dog collar. She almost dropped the flashlight in shock and felt so nauseous that she had to cover her mouth.

"I guess there's a pretty good reason why Clunkers disappeared," John said grimly. "It looks like you were right, Sarah. Let's see what else we can find."

They didn't have to dig too far before they discovered further gory evidence.

"What's this?" Sarah asked, holding up a particularly smelly object.

John shone the flashlight on to it and they both almost retched. It was the rotting hoof of a donkey.

But there was worse to come. John unearthed a skull, its teeth bared in death. There were still some remnants of fur attached to it. "Clunkers," he said. "This is . . . *was* Clunkers."

This time, Sarah really was sick.

They looked at the remains in silence, broken only

by the shushing waves. A seagull cried as if it was mourning for the poor old dog.

"The Sandman *did* kill Clunkers to use him in the sand-sculpture competition. And I bet he killed a real donkey, too. Why else would their remains be hidden together under the pier near his house?" Sarah said angrily. She turned to John. "We have to tell the police — and the competition organizers. They'll ban him for life!"

"I think you're right," said John. "The Sandman did do it. But we've got no *definite* proof that it was the Sandman who put the bones here, do we? And don't forget that all the locals love the Sandman. They won't believe it was him — they'll think that we're just some out-of-towners who are jealous," he finished glumly.

Sarah thought for a moment before speaking. Then she smiled. "Unless we can get them to investigate his new creation," she said.

John looked at her and smiled. "Good point," he said. "We'll tell them tomorrow."

As they emerged from under the pier, Sarah noticed a light on in one of the rooms in the Sandman's house. Had he been watching them?

* * *

It wasn't difficult to find the competition organizers the following morning. The man and two women who ran the competition were on the beach doing press interviews and photos with the town's mayor to promote the event.

When they took a break, John and Sarah ran over to them, the words and accusations tumbling breathlessly out of their mouths.

"The Sandman has been cheating for years!" Sarah insisted. "He kills animals — *real* animals — and just coats them with sand."

"What nonsense is this?" asked the mayor, a ruddy-faced, chubby man with eyebrows like overfed caterpillars. He tried to ignore Sarah and John, but they insisted that the organizers check out the Sandman's sculpture.

"The proof's in his tent!" said John. "We've seen a dead octopus in there. Come and see!"

One or two of the reporters interviewing the organizers and the mayor were listening to this with interest.

"Sounds like a good story," one of them said — and John and Sarah were glad to have them along.

They reached the Sandman's tent and pulled back the canvas door. The Sandman was there, but there was no sea-life sculpture — just a pile of damp sand.

Sarah and John looked at each other in dismay.

"We've been asked to inspect your sculpture," said one of the organizers, looking rather embarrassed. "An octopus, supposedly — and wonderful, too, I'm sure, if it actually existed. We would have ignored the request as it was only from these children — probably mischief makers — but the press were here and —"

"Are you calling us liars?" John interrupted indignantly.

But no one answered him.

The Sandman smiled at the mayor, the organizers, and the reporters. "No need to worry," he said politely. "You're very welcome in here. But as you can see, I haven't even started my work yet. It's still in the planning stages — though I can certainly promise you it won't be an octopus. Children *do* have such vivid imaginations, don't they?"

"We're perfectly capable of using our eyes," Sarah began.

But the mayor snapped, "Enough! You children have caused enough embarrassment here already!"

And then one of the organizers said, "Wait a minute! I remember you two now. You came second in last year's competition. Is this some kind of petty revenge because somebody else beat you?" he said, staring at Sarah and John with a laserlike glare.

All three organizers apologized again, then, after giving John and Sarah extremely dirty looks, disappeared out of the tent.

The mayor turned to Sarah and John. "I'll leave you two in here to apologize to Mr. Bronson!" And he squeezed his tubby frame out of the tent.

Sarah turned defiantly to the Sandman. "We know what you've done," she said, feeling her cheeks burn with anger. "And now you've just taken all that sea life away because you knew we'd found you out."

"*And* we know what you did with Clunkers the year before," John snapped. "And the donkey the year before that — and all those other creatures."

The Sandman hung his head. "You're wrong, you

know, about me killing the animals. I loved them all!" he said. "I truly did. They were all old — and died of natural causes. I just wanted to make them famous for a little while — to preserve their bodies a little longer."

Sarah stared at the Sandman, feeling confused. Was he telling the truth about not harming the animals? But even if he was, he was still a cheat and a liar! "You pretended the sculptures were all your own work, though," she pointed out. "You pretended that you'd started from scratch — made them from just sand and seawater, like everyone else!"

"Yes," the Sandman admitted. "You've caught me, fair and square. But I've an idea for this year that you might be interested in," he said, smiling at them.

Sarah couldn't help staring at his fake, white-teethed smile.

"If you come back here later on and help me create a real, true, sand sculpture," the Sandman continued, "I'll let you enter the finished sculpture in *your* names, whatever we make. You can share the prize money. It's higher than ever this year. I can't be fairer than that, can I? If you like, you could donate it to an animal charity."

Sarah and John looked at each other, unsure what to say.

The Sandman sighed and sat down on the sand. "I'm not really a bad man, you know," he said. He looked up at them with sadness-filled eyes. "Come back later on, and we'll start building as soon as you arrive."

"You'll really let us win?" John asked.

"Yes," the Sandman replied. "I give you my word."

"And you promise to use no more animals?" Sarah asked.

"Cross my heart and hope to die," the Sandman replied earnestly.

The sun was just creeping down toward the horizon when Sarah and John returned to where the Sandman's tent was pitched. They could see the early-evening crowds promenading near the stores, but the beach around them was deserted. A small sliver of light was emanating from the Sandman's tent, so they knew he was inside, waiting for them.

"Here we go," John said to his sister, smiling. "This year will be our year to win!"

Sarah smiled back, and they made their way into the tent.

It was sunny. It was morning. John and Sarah were outside again.

But they couldn't move.

Nor could they scream. Their mouths seemed to be full of sand. They could feel it grating between their teeth. Their arms and legs felt as though they were fixed in concrete.

Nearby they could hear the voices of their parents, talking to the Sandman.

"Such a wonderful sculpture," their mom said. "What amazingly realistic children! You're bound to win again this year."

The Sandman smiled. "Your John and Sarah were my inspiration — I couldn't have done it without them. Truly."

John and Sarah watched through the tiny eyeholes in the sculpture as their parents walked away.

The Sandman stood waving as they disappeared from view.

MAN'S BEST FRIEND

It was the first funeral Ben had ever attended. There were a few other kids there, all looking as uncomfortable as him, trying not to fidget in their hastily bought black clothes, but it was mostly aunts, uncles, and, of course, his parents.

Tears tickled the backs of his eyes, but Ben was determined not to cry. He was twelve, and too old for that, though some of the adults around him were crying. That was the worst part — seeing so many people he knew being upset.

He closed his eyes as his grandfather's coffin was lowered into the open grave. He'd been too nervous to eat breakfast that morning, and his stomach started to grumble, but, luckily, the minister began reading out passages from the Bible in a voice loud enough to drown out anything.

When the minister had finished, Ben's mom walked forward and dropped a single yellow carnation onto the coffin. Ben walked forward and peered into the hole. One day, he thought, he'd be lying in one of those long wooden boxes himself. The thought of it made a shiver creep up his spine.

Ben was dreading the gathering at one of his aunts' houses after the funeral even more than the funeral itself. He knew that everyone would stand around talking awkwardly about his grandfather, and he didn't want to hear it.

But Ben had been wrong. It was far from depressing. Instead of mourning, the family seemed to be celebrating the fact that they were all still alive and together. Many of the older relatives were swapping childhood memories of Eddie Stevens, his grandfather. Ben felt his mood lifting — until one sentence made him stop dead in his tracks.

"Of course, I stopped going there after he got that awful thing!" One of his aunts was speaking, simultaneously nibbling on her turkey sandwich.

What was she talking about? He cocked an ear, trying not to look like he was eavesdropping.

"*Everyone* stopped going there," said another aunt. "I don't know why he bought that horrible creature in the first place. I hated the way its eyes followed you around the room."

The first aunt nodded. "Well, it certainly gave me the creeps. The way it glared at you, it felt like it was trying to get inside your head. I don't know how he lived with it."

Ben wondered if he should ask what they were talking about, but then he saw his mom. She was sitting in an old leather armchair, sobbing into a handkerchief. Dad was sitting on the arm of the chair with his arm around her. Ben couldn't imagine losing *his* dad, and after all, Grandpa had been *her* dad. The thought chased the creature with glaring eyes right out of Ben's head.

Two weeks had passed since the funeral, and Grandpa was still very much on Ben's mind. In fact, Mom and

Dad talked about little else. They'd told him that Grandpa had left a whole house full of stuff, and his landlord wanted it removed by the end of the month. Mom and Dad were so busy trying to sort it all out that they often seemed to forget that Ben was even there.

He'd decided to leave them both alone and just stay out of their way until it was all done. But that morning, his mom came into his room and placed something on his bedside table, saying something about it being what his grandfather had wanted him to have. Ben opened the battered old leather pouch and peered inside. Something old and metallic shone back at him. Pulling it out using the old tarnished chain, he saw that it was an ancient-looking pocket watch. The glass was cracked, and it ticked as loudly as a bomb. Ben noticed that the back was so badly rusted that a fine orange dust came off on his hands. He didn't really want it, but if Grandpa had insisted . . .

Ben felt a wave of guilt wash over him. He hadn't seen Grandpa Eddie too often in the last few years. Whenever Mom and Dad had gone to visit him, Ben had been busy with something else.

Sometimes he'd come up with false excuses, too.

Ben's grandfather hadn't looked after himself or his house too well after Grandma died a few years ago. The house had begun to reek a little; it smelled of unwashed clothes and food that should have been thrown away. When you left, you took that smell with you. So Ben had mostly stayed away. And now it was too late to visit his grandfather again.

"Ben?" His mom's voice made him jump. She was calling from downstairs. "The rest of your grandfather's stuff has arrived. Do you want to come and have a look?"

Ben had been so lost in his thoughts he hadn't even heard the van pull up outside. He grabbed a pair of jeans and a T-shirt from the back of his chair, hurried downstairs and out of the back door, and saw that Rex had already beaten him to it, running outside and barking excitedly at the large truck in the driveway.

Rex was Ben's huge German shepherd, with a gray-brown back, creamy belly, long legs, and a bushy tail. Rex had been a stray, rescued from the local animal shelter. Mom and Dad had taken Ben along, and he'd been allowed to pick which dog he wanted. Rather than one of the small, cute puppies, Ben had chosen Rex.

Rex was pretty scary if you didn't know him well, especially when he launched into all-out Bark Mode. With Rex around, you didn't need burglar alarms.

The van was massive. It filled the entire driveway and looked big enough to transport the contents of an entire apartment building, not just Grandpa's collection of stuff.

Ben caught his reflection in the wing mirror as the driver unfastened the back doors. His mom had made him get a haircut for the funeral, and he wished it would grow back more quickly. He ran his hand through it, trying to spike it up.

"Let's get to work," said his dad.

Ben went around the back and looked inside, casting his eye over the entire worldly goods and possessions of Edward Stevens, deceased.

Or, to put it another way — a great big heap of useless old junk.

Ben peered inside. The van was filled with yellowing newspapers, rusty old toasters, and similar garbage.

Compared to most of this stuff, the pocket watch seemed top quality. "What are we supposed to do with it all?" he asked.

His dad put his hands on his hips. "See what's fit for keeping, what's worth giving to charity, and what's only good for throwing away, I suppose." He stood back and looked at the huge pile of ragtag items. "It's mostly junk, Ben — but the landlord wanted us to move everything right after the funeral. Otherwise I guess we'd have trashed most of it at Grandpa's house."

"Some of it's OK," Ben said. He'd spotted several cool relics: odd little ornaments, a tray full of old stamps, a prehistoric-looking typewriter, and a radio — or *wireless* as Grandpa always called it — which looked absolutely ancient. He'd seen TV shows where people sold antiques for a fortune. Maybe some things were worth keeping.

Rex shared Ben's enthusiasm. He bounded up into the van, excited.

Ben smiled. He knew that for Rex, this was Sniffing Heaven.

His dad picked up a box from on top of a dressing table and handed it to Ben. "Look in here," he said.

It was full of old photos. Some were fully developed, some just negatives or postage stamp–sized contact prints. Nobody had even *thought* of digital cameras back when these were taken. Some of the prints were curled up and cracked. Some had been gnawed at by silverfish and attacked by mold. But many were just fine. Ben flicked through them. One showed Grandpa and Grandma together when they were young, on the beach, wearing old-fashioned bathing suits.

Ben's dad looked over his shoulder and laughed. "We have to keep those," he said.

"But they smell weird, Dad," Ben said. "I could scan them all onto a CD. Then we could keep them forever. Mom would like that."

"Nice thought, Ben, but I don't think it's the photos we are smelling," Dad said, nodding to the back of the van.

His dad was right. The awful smell seemed to be coming from beneath a large bedsheet.

Ben clambered over Rex and reached out to pull off the sheet. A loud *squaaaaawk* made him jerk away his hand. He shrieked with shock, almost tripping backward over his own feet. "What's that?" he said, his heart whacking against his rib cage.

He stepped back to let his dad pull away the sheet.

Underneath was an extraordinarily beautiful brass birdcage. Its golden bars twisted in spiral patterns, and tiny windows of colored glass were fixed into them. The hook at the top was carved into the shape of a dragon. The roof was crafted with intricate patterns, too.

But what lurked inside wasn't so beautiful.

Rex pelted out of the van as if his tail was on fire, knocking Ben backward onto the seat of a dusty, old chair. He peered into the cage.

A parrot? he said to himself.

That's what it was, though if it hadn't squawked, he'd have thought it was dead, stuffed, and chewed by moths.

The parrots Ben had seen on nature programs were beautiful things with bright, sparkling eyes, shiny, clean feathers, and more vivid splashes of color than a fireworks display. Not this one. It was gnarled and ugly, and there was way too much of it. It nearly filled the cage, but it wasn't puffing its feathers out or anything like that — it didn't have many feathers. Most of its body seemed to be covered in scars, and what few feathers it did have were ragged and gray. The breathing holes on either side of its beak looked like they had been drilled by a blindfolded carpenter. And its sharp claws, wrapped around the perch, looked like they could clamp deep into your flesh and remove a huge chunk of it with no effort at all.

"Meet Igor," his dad said.

"Igor?" Ben said. "What kind of name's that?"

"Well, what did you expect him to be called?" his dad laughed. "Tinkerbell?"

Ben's dad was right. Igor was a suitably scary name for a very scary-looking bird.

"You know, this little fella was your grandfather's best friend in the last few months of his life," said his dad. "I think he bought it at a flea market somewhere. He'd been told all sorts of stories about it, that it was at least a hundred years old and might live much longer."

To Ben, the thing looked like it had actually died

about a hundred years ago, but just hadn't realized it yet. He didn't like it at all. He particularly didn't like the way it was staring at him, twisting its head around so that one black eye was fixed firmly on his face.

"Grandpa told your mom that Igor's a good talker," Dad said, rapping on the bars with a finger. "Pretty Polly, pretty Polly."

"Careful, Dad, he'll bite off your finger," Ben warned.

But his dad was too busy trying to get the bird to talk. "Pretty Polly, pretty Polly."

Luckily, it didn't peck him. But it didn't speak, either. It just made a low, clucking noise, followed by a sandpaperlike rasping sound.

"Oh, well, if we keep it and it gets to like us," Dad said, "I'm sure it'll start talking eventually."

Now it wasn't just the parrot that was lost for words. Ben could hardly believe his ears. *Keep* it? He had to be kidding.

"Don't worry." Dad smiled. "I'm just joking. I wouldn't dream of it. Your mom might take some convincing, though. She knows how much Igor meant to your grandfather."

* * *

Ben didn't want to share his home with the mean-looking bird, so he spent some time in his room, surfing the Internet, looking for bad facts about parrots to show his mom. Most of the parrot sites he found were by parrot lovers, but he still found a few good quotes:

Parrots are noisy, messy, potentially destructive, costly to purchase and keep, and need lots of time and attention.

All parrots will bite their owners under certain conditions.

Parrots can be aggressive and may become excited, hiss, screech, flap their wings, and attack if they consider a person to be a threat to them.

He printed out what he found and took the sheet of paper downstairs.

The parrot's cage was already in the kitchen. Igor was crouched on his perch, with Ben's parents taking turns to feed him segments of orange through the bars. In return, the bird made grateful clucking noises and held its head so Ben's mom could reach a finger through the bars and rub its chin.

There was something weird about the scene. The parrot was horrible to look at and potentially violent, so why were they cooing over it like it was a cute little kitten? In the van, his dad had seemed to dislike it just as much as he did.

Maybe they were just pleased because Igor had finally started talking to them.

"*Who's a pretty boy, then? Who's a pretty boy?*" Igor said in a freaky singsong voice.

"Not you, buddy," Ben said under his breath. "That's for sure."

"See, he's quite friendly," said Dad, smiling.

"Yes, sweet old thing," said Mom.

Sweet? How could they see all those scars on its body and not turn away? How could they smell it and not rush to the sink to throw up? Had the bedraggled old bird hypnotized them with those bulging black eyes?

"*Who's a pretty boy?*" it repeated.

"Poor old Igor looks like he's on his last legs, anyway," Dad said. "He won't live for much longer. Maybe we should keep him till then. For Grandpa's sake."

"Oh, that's the least we can do," Mom agreed.

Ben waved his piece of paper. "But it might attack us. It says here."

"Attack us?" Dad laughed. "A canary with its wings

tied behind its back could beat this old fellow up. Poor thing."

Ben tried Mom instead. "You can't have a thing like that flapping about the house," he said. "Imagine if its claws got caught up in your hair."

Mom fed the bird another segment of orange. "Igor won't be flapping about the house, silly," she said, smiling. "He'll be in a cage. But we'll sleep on it and decide what to do in the morning. For tonight, though, let's put the cage in the living room."

The *living room*?

Had Ben heard her right? He'd been hoping that they'd keep it outside in the garage, although the field behind the back garden would have been preferable. And Mom didn't even let Rex in the living room, so why this parrot? She was so proud of that room and kept it so spotlessly clean and tidy that Ben was surprised she even let *him* in it. It didn't make sense.

He watched open-mouthed as Dad moved the cage and its stand into the best room of the house.

After installing Igor in the living room, Ben's dad disappeared off into his study, and his mom ran out to the supermarket to do some shopping for dinner. That left Ben alone with the creature.

He hated it being in the house at all, let alone the living room, and he didn't want to go anywhere near it, but it was time for his favorite TV show. *So I guess I have to put up with it*, he thought. *For now*.

Ben walked into the room and sat on the floor. He turned on the TV and placed his plate on his lap. While his mom was out, he'd taken the opportunity to sneak in a sandwich and a glass of milk. Food wasn't allowed in the living room, and Mom's eyes had built-in crumb detectors. She always kept the room perfect in case they had visitors. Ben looked around at the spotless rug spread across the floor, the polished table and bookcase, the neatly pleated curtains at the window, and the big, expensive sofa and chairs. It seemed so weird that she'd allowed that moth-eaten, smelly old bird in there.

The brass cage had been placed next to the tallest lamp, which Mom always kept on because she said it was cheaper than using the main lights. Igor was a big bird and cast a menacing shadow across the wall.

Ben was sure he could feel the bird's eyes burning

into him from behind as he watched TV, but he was determined not to look at it. As the opening music started and the credits rolled, Ben decided that there was no way he was going to let Igor spoil his favorite show.

"Squawkkkkkkkkkkkkkkkk! Squawwwwwwwwwwwkkkkk!"

It sounded as though Igor had been strapped to the most dangerous roller coaster in the world and had been sent down the deepest dip at top speed.

At first, Ben tried to ignore it. He guessed that the bird just wanted attention, and it certainly wouldn't be getting any from him. He remembered reading on one of the parrot Web sites that the birds were like toddlers, and if you ignored them when they threw a tantrum, they eventually got bored and stopped being noisy. If you didn't, they could become permanent screamers. So he reckoned that when Igor finally realized that he wasn't listening, it'd shut its stupid beak.

But every time an actor spoke, the parrot screeched louder, and every word of dialogue was lost. Ben used the remote control to put subtitles up, but the program was still impossible to enjoy.

Then the first commercial break arrived, and the parrot finally shut up. Peace at last. Ben suddenly got a cold feeling down his back. Why was the bird being quiet now? Surely Igor couldn't tell what was a program and what was an ad? Then the thought hit him like a punch: *It's only interested in spoiling my program.* Sure enough, proof came when the show began again, and it immediately resumed squawking.

Ben couldn't take it anymore. He turned around and yelled at the parrot. "Shut up! Just shut up!"

The bird stopped, mid-squawk, and fell silent.

Ben smiled. At least it realized who was boss now. He settled back down on the sofa and tried to get back into his program.

Then he heard a low voice from behind him. *"I killed your grandpa."*

Ben's heart froze in his chest. He turned slowly, the show forgotten.

The parrot stood on its perch, head twisted to one side, its left eye fixed on Ben. Not a healthy eye like parrots should have, but an unhealthy, runny-looking eye like the yolk of a big, greasy fried egg.

Ben clicked the MUTE button on the remote. The room was quiet now. He could hear his mom in the kitchen, back from shopping and slicing carrots on her wooden chopping board, and a car whooshing past the front of the house, and some kids shouting and laughing in the next street.

He rose and walked slowly toward the cage. His throat felt like it was shrinking to the size of a pinhole, but somehow he managed a strangled whisper. "What did you say?"

The bird shuffled on its perch, then nuzzled up to the bars. *"You heard,"* it said. *"I killed your grandpa."*

There was no mistaking what the freaky singsong voice had said this time. Ben dashed out of the living room and into the kitchen, where he found his dad helping Mom with the cooking. "Mom! Dad!" he shouted. "The bird — it spoke!"

"'Course he did, sweetie." Mom smiled. "Parrots talk. You know that. He was talking to us in the kitchen before you came down."

"But you don't know what it said. . . ." Ben stammered.

"What did he say?" Dad asked inquisitively. "All we could get out of him was, '*Who's a pretty boy*?'"

There was an air of anticipation as Mom and Dad waited for Ben's reply.

"It said that it killed Grandpa," Ben said.

Mom's eyes widened like saucers.

Dad looked angry. "How could you say that, especially in front of your mom?" he snapped.

"But it did," Ben insisted. "That's what it said!"

Dad must have realized that Ben was genuinely upset. "Ben," he said more gently, "that's impossible. We all know that parrots can talk, but they only repeat what they've heard. Check those parrot facts of yours."

"That's right, sweetie," Mom said. "They can only imitate. They can't start conversations."

"But that's what it said!" Ben insisted. Why didn't they believe him?

"You probably heard something on your TV show," Dad suggested. "One of the characters said those words and you just thought it was the parrot."

"But there's nothing on the TV show about someone's grandpa being killed," Ben said, "so how could the TV say that?"

"Well, if Igor did say anything like that, he was just

imitating something he'd heard somewhere else," Mom said. "Your grandpa kept Igor in his own living room, so he could watch TV with him. Parrots have long memories, you know. And you know what Grandpa was like — he never turned off the TV. Igor has probably watched thousands of films and TV shows. So he was just repeating what he heard on one of them."

"Well, I'm not going back in the living room," Ben protested. "Can't we just get rid of Igor?"

"I knew it," said Ben's mom, sounding upset. "You didn't like Igor from the moment you saw him and you're just saying all this to make us get rid of him. What would Grandpa have said?"

"All right, forget it," Ben said. "Keep the bird. See if I care. I've only lived here twelve years and that thing's been here a whole hour. So put Igor first."

He stomped out of the kitchen, into the hall, and up the stairs. He wouldn't watch TV anymore. He'd just stay in his room and read comics, and leave his parents downstairs with the parrot. If they liked it so much, it could take his place at dinner, too, for all he cared. Maybe he'd refuse to come down at all until it had gone. That would show them.

Rex was waiting outside his room, whimpering. Ben had never seen him like that before. "Rex? Boy? Are you OK?" Ben asked, kneeling down and stroking the dog's head. "You hate that thing, too, don't you, boy?"

But it was more than Rex just *hating* Igor. The way he'd pelted out of the van suggested he was scared. It was as if Rex had sensed that the bird was bad news from the first second he saw it. As if he *knew*. After all, dogs were supposed to be more sensitive than humans about certain things — able to detect things that people couldn't.

It was still weird. Igor was just a bird in a cage, and Rex was a great big dog.

"Don't worry, boy, it'll be gone soon," Ben said.

He spread a selection of comics across his bed and tried to lose himself in a story. But the thumping of his heart stopped him from concentrating. And he couldn't forget what the parrot had said.

I killed your grandpa.

Could it be true? Dad had said the parrot had been Grandpa's best friend. Could it really have killed him? And if so, how?

He lay back on his bed, covered his face with the open pages of his comic, and closed his eyes. He had to think about this. . . .

The dream started almost immediately. Ben was back at Grandpa's funeral, hot and itchy and stuffed into that new and uncomfortable black suit, surrounded by his relatives and listening to the minister read from the Bible.

But something was different.

The old gray parrot was perched on Grandpa's tombstone, watching them all and *laughing*.

Laughing like crazy. And repeating the minister's words in its mocking singsong voice.

And no matter how loud the minister read, the parrot boomed louder, its cackling ringing around the graveyard like sinister church bells. But nobody seemed to notice or hear it but Ben.

Then, as the minister said "Rest in peace," the parrot opened its scraggy wings and came for Ben, hurtling through the air.

Ben threw himself to the ground, but the parrot dived down, swooping toward him like a guided missile. It scored a hit with its claws. They felt razor-sharp and Ben screamed, but nobody around him seemed to notice what was happening. The minister just carried on reading.

Ben put a hand to his chest, feeling the blood coursing through his fingers. . . .

And then he woke up. He sat upright like he'd been zapped with electricity, his hands clutching at his chest.

He realized that he'd been dreaming, but his hand still felt sticky. He hardly dared look at it. But there was no blood. All that glistened on his fingers was dog spit. Rex was by his bedside. The big dog must have woken him up by licking his hand when his arm was dangling over the bed.

"Good boy," Ben whispered.

Even though his stomach was growling, Ben refused to go downstairs. He tried reading to calm himself down, but his whole body was shaking. He just couldn't forget about Igor. He had to find out whether the parrot had really said what he thought it had.

And, if it had, whether or not it was true.

* * *

It was early the next morning, and the sun was barely up. Ben waited until he was sure that his parents were still asleep, building up his bravado. *It's just a bird, nothing but an old bird*, he kept telling himself.

When he'd summoned up enough courage, he went downstairs, his pace getting slower with each step, because each step took him closer to the living room. Closer to the parrot's lair. He stood outside the closed door for what seemed like ages.

It's now or never, he thought finally, and turned the handle.

To his surprise, his mom was in the room feeding Igor a piece of carrot through the bars of its cage. She was trying to get it to talk. "Carrot, mmmmm, carrot, mmmmmm," she said. "Hello, good morning, hello, good morning."

This wasn't good. Ben knew the parrot would never repeat what it had told him in front of his mom. Something told him that those words were meant for him alone.

Ben was about to speak — but then his jaw dropped open, and all that managed to escape his lips was a disbelieving gasp. He stared around the room, hardly able to believe what he was seeing. Dirt, and plenty of it, in Mom's clean, spotless, always-kept-perfect-for-visitors living room. The mess was a mixture of feathers and sawdust. It had spilled out of the cage and was piled around the stand on the carpet.

His mom was trying to get Igor to recite a limerick. "There once was a pretty old parrot, who lived on a diet of carrot. . . ."

Igor remained as silent as death itself.

"Mom, look at this," Ben said.

"Look at what?" his mom asked. "Can't you see I'm feeding Igor?"

Ben bent down and scooped up a handful of the litter. He held it out to her. "The dirt! The mess!"

He quickly regretted handling it. It wasn't just sawdust and feathers in his fingers. He could feel something else in there, too. Bird poop. He threw it back down on to the carpet in disgust.

"Oh, grow up, Ben," Mom said. "A little speck or two of dirt never hurt anyone."

Ben's jaw dropped even farther. Could this really be the same woman who would go crazy if Rex so much as poked his head in the living room door? The same woman who hadn't stopped complaining for a week when Ben had brushed some crumbs off his sweater and they'd landed on the living room carpet?

She continued feeding the bird. She'd already forgotten about Ben. "Carrot, mmmm, carrot, mmm —"

"Are you sure it wouldn't prefer organic ones?" Ben said sarcastically. "They're supposed to taste better, and you obviously think Igor should be treated like a king."

"Oh, yes, don't they sell them at the supermarket?" Mom said.

Ben couldn't believe it. She was taking him seriously! Normally, she said that organic food was too expensive, but it appeared that nothing was too good for Igor.

"We'd better go out and stock up on more food for him. He's got such a healthy appetite. And we should get him some toys, too. Do you want to come?"

Ben could hardly believe that he was starting to feel jealous of a parrot. "No, thanks. I'll stay here," he said. "In case Igor wants anything. He might get an itch that wants scratching, or need someone to change the channel on the TV."

Ben's mom smiled, still not detecting any sarcasm in

Ben's voice. "Now you're being sensible," she said. "I knew you'd grow to like Igor eventually." She left the room and called his dad. "Joe? We're going shopping for Igor. Ben said we should get some organic carrots for him. It's still early, but I think that the supermarket on the other side of town is open."

"Great idea!" Ben's dad said. "I'll be right down."

Ben couldn't believe his ears. His father hated shopping and came up with any excuse to get out of it — even if it meant washing the car for the second time in a weekend. But at least now Ben had his chance.

He waited until he heard the back door click shut and the car drive away. His mom and dad were gone. It was time.

He stood in front of the parrot cage.

The bird cocked its head to one side, as if listening for instructions from evil, invisible spirits. It stood high on its perch now, its whole body fully alert, as if it knew that Ben was a threat. Seeming to swell, and staring right back at him.

But Ben didn't back down. "What did you say to me yesterday?" he said.

Igor strutted back and forth on its perch but said nothing.

"Go on, you stupid bird — speak!" Ben demanded.

As Igor remained silent, Ben's confidence returned, swelling in his chest like a balloon. It was just a normal parrot. Of course it was. How could he have thought otherwise? He'd imagined the whole thing, that was how, and he smiled at how silly he'd been. But as Ben turned to leave, the eerie, singsong voice cut through the silence like a sword.

"I killed your grandpa!"

Ben swung back to face the old bird. He'd been right all along! What Igor had said yesterday had been for real.

The parrot stared him out, the size of its pupils growing larger and smaller. That was a sign of aggression; Ben had read so on the Internet.

"And you're next!" it screeched.

Ben felt waves of shock roll over him.

The parrot looked Ben up and down, letting out a nasty little chuckle. *"A scrawny little scrap of flesh and blood like you. No trouble, no trouble."*

Ben only knew one thing for sure. He had to get out of the house *right now*. The best thing to do, he reckoned, was to take Rex for a walk.

It was a beautiful morning — blue skies and wispy clouds everywhere. After several calls, Rex emerged, slinking nervously down the stairs. The big dog didn't even wait for Ben to put on his leash. The moment Ben opened the door, he shot out.

"Don't worry, boy," Ben said. "We'll get as far away from that thing as we can."

It wasn't fun walking at first because Rex was straining so hard on the leash. But the farther from the house and from Igor they got, the more he began to settle down. Finally, his confidence returned, and he relaxed back into doing regular dog things — sniffing at the local dogs, inspecting lumps of grass, lampposts, puddles, trees, and everything else in his path, as if he didn't have a care in the world.

Ben and Rex walked and walked down the tree-lined streets, stopping only for traffic, and never once looking back. Ben felt his own fear begin to wear off a little, too. The peacefulness of the neighborhood seemed to work its way through his skin and calm him down. He suddenly noticed what a nice day it was. One of those lazy summer afternoons where the sun gently warms your face as you walk.

It was a nice area. Sometimes he found it a bit boring, but a big part of him knew he was lucky to live there. The streets were clean. There wasn't much traffic. Most of the neighbors seemed friendly. A deep sense of weirdness had invaded his life since Igor had arrived, but out here, the sheer *normality* of everything was reassuring.

And everything *was* going on as normal. People were taking out their trash, washing their cars, cutting their lawns, and sharing cups of coffee and gardening tips over their garden fences. It was as if the whole deal with the parrot had just been a nightmare, and reality had suddenly clicked back into place.

Ben knew that his mom and dad were right. Parrots aren't like humans. They can't make up conversations. They can only mimic human speech signals, the same way they mimic ringing phones or passing ice-cream trucks. That's the deal. To them, it's just noise. They don't know what they're saying. So Ben couldn't have heard what he did coming out of that parrot's beak, either today or yesterday. Unless Igor *had* picked up all that dialogue from some old film or TV show — but what were the chances of that?

They reached the park and Ben sat down under a tree, idly rubbing a piece of grass between his fingers, trying to make sense of it all. He lay back and looked at the clouds drifting past. Some of them resembled things: everything from a giraffe to his dad's car. One of them looked just like a wide-open jagged bird beak. . . .

Suddenly, there was a tongue in his face, and foul breath filling both his nostrils. He sprang up from the ground in alarm. But it was just Rex, licking his face.

"OK, OK, I'm clean now," Ben laughed, wrestling in the grass with his dog. He felt really grateful that Rex was around.

"I'm *not* crazy, am I, boy?" he said, realizing something important. "You're proof of that because you're just as scared of that old bird as I am. *You* know the truth about Igor, too."

Rex dipped his head to one side as if listening carefully, which made Ben laugh.

He chose to pass through the churchyard on the way home. He wanted to look at Grandpa's grave. When they had buried him, the headstone hadn't been finished yet. He ambled through the sprawling maze of tombstones. It was an old cemetery, with some really interesting old stones and markers, many of them leaning and eroded from centuries of storms. Some of the names on the older stones had worn away completely. Plenty of creepy old statues of angels and cherubs were dotted between them.

Rex was more interested in the uncut grass and the old trees that dropped their wormy apples on the ground around them.

Finally, Ben found what he was looking for. He stood and read the headstone, while Rex plonked himself down, panting happily.

EDWARD STEVENS
BELOVED FATHER AND GRANDFATHER
REST IN PEACE

Ben thought about Grandpa. His house might have been full of junk, but he was a great old guy, and he did miss him a lot. Had the parrot really killed him?

Only you know the truth about that bird, Grandpa, he thought, *and there's no way you can tell me.*

Rex started acting strangely again as soon as they arrived back in Ben's street, his head bowed down low and his tail drooping. By the time they reached the house, Ben had to drag him through the gate into the front yard.

"Don't worry, boy, there's nothing to be scared of," he said, though he didn't sound very convincing — he knew all too well that there was *plenty* to be scared of.

But no matter how hard Ben tugged, Rex wouldn't go into the house. He point-blank refused. And when Ben tried too hard to force him, he actually curled his top lip and gave a little growl.

"All right, all right," Ben said, and let go.

As soon as he did, Rex pelted around the side of the house to the end of the long backyard and lay there, cowering under a hedge.

Ben entered the house by himself.

His mom and dad were in the kitchen, preparing what appeared to be dinner — until Ben took a closer look at the ingredients.

Most of the food on the table was pellets. Disgusting-looking bird pellets. Brown ones and brightly colored, fruit-shaped ones. Pellets on plates, pellets in saucers, pellets in bowls. The pellets made the sunflower seeds and cuttlebones in the other dishes look tasty.

It was all food for Igor.

Not all of it was spread across the tables. Some of it was bubbling and boiling on the stove. The room looked more like a mad scientist's laboratory than a kitchen.

Ben's mom was grinding a mixture of pellets and seeds together in a big tub. His dad stood next to her, shelling nuts. There was something weird about them both. They looked as blank-faced as sleepwalkers.

"Igor will enjoy shelling those nuts for himself," Ben's mom snapped at his dad, "so leave them alone. Here's something you can do."

She poured some orange juice into a bowl. Ben read the label: FRESHLY SQUEEZED ORGANIC ORANGE JUICE

"Dip some of the pellets in that," Mom told Dad. "It'll taste nicer for him."

Ben was amazed. She never bought organic, freshly squeezed orange juice for *him* to drink. But she'd bought the expensive, healthy stuff for Igor, just to dip in pellets!

For a few seconds, Ben was speechless. "Dad," he said. "It's Rex. He won't come in the house. He's too scared because of that bird. He's in the yard now, and he won't budge."

Dad looked annoyed that Ben was distracting him from his pellet-dipping. "Well, we don't really need Rex anymore, do we?" he said. "We've got Igor now. I don't know why we ever let that dog in the house in the first place. I'm thinking about taking him back to the shelter next week. He's more trouble than he's worth."

Ben couldn't believe what he was hearing. "Dad, how can you say that?" he said. Ben's dad had always loved Rex. They were like best friends. Dad would spend hours playing with him in the backyard. Sometimes he and Ben would argue about whose turn it was to take him for a walk.

"Easily," Dad said. "That horrible old mutt probably has fleas, anyway, so he's better off living outside."

Mom nodded. "Two pets is one too many," she said. "And Rex would be much happier back in the shelter with all the other dirty, slobbering, flea-ridden hounds."

"You *can't* take him back to the shelter," Ben cried. "I love Rex even if *you* don't!" He was so angry now he wanted to smash the furniture. He didn't dare do that, so he banged his fist on the kitchen table. "And look at this gunk!" he snapped, pointing to the mess of pellets. "What about *our* meal?"

"It's much more convenient if we all eat what Igor eats," Mom said. Ben made a face like he'd already put some of it in his mouth.

There were also some fresh fruit and vegetables spread around the table. He hoped that Mom meant that *they* were what they'd all be sharing, and not the pellets. But there was no way he wanted to share a meal with that bird anyway, no matter what the food was. He couldn't even stand sharing the house with it.

Everything had gone too far. He had to find something out and he had to do it right away. He burst into the living room, stormed across the room, and rattled Igor's cage. "OK, if you killed my grandpa, how did you do it?" he insisted. "Come on. What did you do?"

The parrot looked at Ben and cocked its head.

"Knocked him down the stairs. Feeble old man. Snap went his bones."

Terror ripped its way up from Ben's belly, pushing out of his mouth in a strangled gasp. He ran out of the room. The parrot's words, *"SNAP, SNAP, SNAP,"* matched his footsteps.

Ben slammed the living room door behind him and leaned against it, listening to the parrot's cackle of laughter.

Back in the kitchen, Mom was arranging pellets in a pretty pattern on a plate. Ben sidled up to her.

"Mom," he said quietly. "How did Grandpa die?"

She looked at him strangely. For a brief second, she almost seemed like she'd returned to normal. "He fell downstairs, Ben," she said, sounding sad. Then her face turned back into a frosty mask and she continued arranging the pellets.

Ben's heart sank. Now he knew that Igor had been telling the truth about killing Grandpa. And that meant the parrot might also have been telling the truth when it had said to Ben: *You're next.*

Ben excused himself from the bizarre dinner his mom and dad had prepared. He made himself a sandwich and ate it upstairs. Luckily there was still some real food in the house, so he had peanut butter and jelly instead of pellet sandwiches. Normally, his parents wouldn't have allowed him to eat upstairs or have sandwiches for a main meal. Now they didn't seem to care. They didn't seem to care about *him*, either. As the hours passed, they didn't call to see how he was, where he was, or to ask him to come down and watch TV with them like they usually did. He hardly ever wanted to watch the things they did, but it was nice to be asked. Now, it was as if he didn't exist anymore.

He went downstairs to say good night. A storm had begun, the rain rattling against the glass in the windows so hard that it sounded like someone was throwing pebbles at it.

Ben thought of Rex. Was he still out there? In *that*?

He hurried into the kitchen and turned the key in the back door. The wind was so strong that it almost tugged him outside. He waited for Rex to run in out of the terrible weather, but the big dog didn't come up from the depths of the yard.

"REX!" Ben shouted, his voice tinged with fear. "REX! Are you there, boy?" Still nothing. Ben grabbed an umbrella from the stand by the door and went out into the rain.

One of the shadows at the far end of the yard moved. It was Rex. He was lying down, sinking into the oozing mud that had been soil just a few hours before, the rain bouncing off his fur. Even though Rex was covered in thick hair, Ben could see that he was shivering.

"Come on, boy — come with me," Ben coaxed, opening his dad's shed door. He went inside and lay some sheets on the floor to give Rex somewhere more comfortable to sleep. Rex pushed past Ben and sat at the far end of the shed, backing into the shadows as best he could. After making sure that the dog was warm enough, Ben headed back up toward the house.

He was soaked when he got back inside. Though he really didn't want to, he decided he'd just say a quick good night to his parents, and walked across the kitchen to the living room. His fingers closed over the doorknob, turned it, and gently pushed open the door. He stuck his head inside.

"Good n—" he began, but shock whipped the breath right out of him and he couldn't finish. His eyes bulged from their sockets as they scanned Mom's precious living room.

All the lights were off, but Ben saw what he did from the glowing flicker of the TV. His parents sat in the darkness, staring at it like zombies. Igor was perched on the back of the ripped and chewed sofa with them. The other chairs were chewed, too. As chewed as one of Rex's old rubber bones. So was the rug. So were the lampshades. So were the curtains.

It looked more like an animal cage at the zoo than the best room in the house. The carpet had more sawdust spread across it than a circus ring and sticking out of that sawdust was lots of half-chewed food and parrot droppings.

Ben began to fear for his parents. Had they lost their minds? And more worryingly, he didn't just fear for them; he realized that he felt a little afraid *of* them, too.

"Night, then," Ben said.

They just sat there, the glow of the TV program bouncing off their blank faces. Neither spoke.

Since his mom had made him have his hair cut, Ben was always trying to make it spike up, but he didn't need to do that anymore. The hair on his head was standing on end all by itself.

Ben had to think carefully. He had to think smart, and he had to think fast. That bird had killed his grandfather and now it planned to do the same to him. A day had passed since Igor had said, *"And you're next!"* so Ben reckoned that it had had plenty of time to think about how to do it.

He was worried for his mom and dad, but he thought they'd be safe — for now — because Igor was using them as slaves. Ben was sure that the parrot had hypnotized them to do its bidding. They were in town again at that moment, buying more food for it, and the stores had only just opened.

His mom and dad might be safe, but a kid like him was just in Igor's way — *collateral damage*.

Ben knew he had to get rid of it first — but how?

Could he poison its food?

That was risky, as Mom and Dad were now sharing Igor's meals. Ben didn't want them harmed, too. He hoped that as soon as Igor was gone, his parents would return to normal.

Another idea entered Ben's mind. What if he gave the bird its freedom?

It might just work. . . .

He had to seize his chance while his parents were out of the house.

He entered the living room, making a face as soon as he was through the door. The room stank of dirty parrot. Mom's potpourri bowl on the mantelpiece was supposed to make the room smell nice, but now it was full of bird droppings. And that wasn't the worst of it.

Yesterday's newspaper was torn to shreds and lying like confetti across the sofa. Rotting pieces of lettuce were stuck between the cushions. The flowers in the vases had been snapped off at the stems.

Good work, Igor, he thought, crossing the room, *but soon enough this room — and our lives — will be back to normal. And you'll be gone.*

His plan was to take the cage and leave it outside in the garden with its door open. Surely Igor would fly away. Ben was sure that the parrot wouldn't be able to resist.

The bird watched Ben curiously as he struggled to pick up the big, old cage. It shuffled to and fro on its perch as he carried it out of the living room and into the kitchen.

The cage was heavy and Ben felt his back straining as he moved it. The parrot was much fatter than it had been when it arrived. That was no surprise, Ben thought, as his parents seemed to be spending their entire weekly budget on parrot food. He just hoped that Igor hadn't become too large to fly away.

As he imagined Igor soaring over the rooftops, never to return, he wondered how his folks would react to finding their new pet gone, and how he'd explain it to them.

He'd think of something. He'd say he was cleaning the cage and had accidentally left the back door open, then, before he'd realized it, Igor had flown out. They might believe that, but if Ben was truthful with himself, he knew that he didn't care how angry they'd be. Any punishment would be worth it to see the last of this evil creature.

He left the cage on the kitchen table while he opened the back door. Then he put the cage outside on the doorstep, puffing as he lowered it, and opened the cage door wide.

He stood and waited. Would it work?

The fear that it wouldn't became a low, steady throb in his stomach. "Off you go, Igor," he shouted. "Fly away!"

But Igor didn't move.

"You're free now," Ben said, exasperated. "Free to fly back wherever you came from. Free to go wherever you want." *And with a bit of luck, maybe some hunter will mistake you for a duck or something and shoot you down dead right out of the sky when you're flying overhead.*

But Igor still didn't move.

Ben rattled the cage with his foot. "Are you glued to the perch?" he said. "Fly away, stupid bird. You're free."

The parrot turned and stared at Ben, letting out a low squawk, which sounded more like a nasty chuckle.

"Just what Grandpa tried. And look where he *is now."*

Ben's heart felt like a tree limb that had been snapped in half by a streak of lightning. Igor knew exactly what Ben was trying to do and had no intention of leaving.

Ben kicked the bars of the cage. "Fly," he demanded. "Fly away!"

Igor didn't budge. But this time, Ben wasn't going to take no for an answer. He took the cage farther outsidc, its door swinging on its hinge. He put it down on the concrete, then hurried down the yard. He knew what he needed.

Dad used bamboo canes to prop up the heavy flower blossoms on some of his plants, to stop them from getting broken if there was a storm. Ben looked at them all, standing in a line. They did their job well. After that terrible storm last night, every last one of Dad's hydrangeas was still standing. But would they work on Igor?

He pulled one of the sticks out of the soil. The plant and blossoms that were tied around it sagged, but he doubted that Dad cared about *them* anymore. All he cared about now was Igor.

He ran back to the parrot cage, waving the bamboo cane like a sword. That revolting bird already had more scars on its body than most doctors saw in a lifetime, and if it refused to leave the cage, it would end up with even more. "Are you going to get out or not?" he said.

Igor stayed on its perch.

"OK," Ben said.

He slid the cane through the bars of the cage and started to poke at the parrot.

Jab.

"Go on!"

Jab. Jab.

"Fly! Get out!"

Jabjabjabjabjab.

The parrot moved fast. In one swift movement, it pulled the cane inside the cage and snapped it in half with its beak.

"Next, your spine!" Igor screeched like a drag car with faulty brakes. *"Ready or not, here I come!"*

A surge of terror gripped Ben. Now all he wanted was to keep Igor firmly *inside* the cage. He ran around and slammed the cage door shut, fastening the lock just before the furious bird's talons could tear his fingers off. From inside the cage, it slashed and bit violently at the brass bars.

"Time to die! Time to die!"

Ben hurried to the shed to grab a pair of his dad's thick gardening gloves. There was no way he'd touch that cage again without those on. He found Rex in there, cowering on thc papers he'd laid out the night before. He stroked the dog's head in passing.

Once he had located the gloves, he headed back to the cage. His heart pounding like voodoo drums, Ben tried to lug it back inside. The bird grew wilder and wilder. It tried its best to snap the bars in half with its beak and lunged repeatedly at Ben's gloved hands.

As Ben managed to reposition the cage next to the now torn-up lamp, it screamed again and again. *"Time to die!"* it shouted, staring at him with one yellowing eye. *"Your turn! Your turn!"*

Ben did his best to ignore the terrifying threat and hurried back outside. He ran to the shed and threw off the gloves and saw that Rex was crouching under the worktable.

"Come on, boy," Ben said. But Rex would only back farther into the shadow.

Ben crouched down and held out his hand. Rcx ventured forward and licked it. But even in that moment, Ben could faintly hear the evil parrot's deathly lullaby squawking.

"Time to die . . . very soon!"

* * *

That night as Ben lay in bed, every little sound made him jump. The squeak of floorboards from his parents' room as they prepared for bed. The tapping of tiny moth wings and feet against the bedroom window. The gurgle of the pipes in the walls. The house creaking in all its secret places. But he tried hard to concentrate. Now he knew he was in serious danger; he had to figure out what to do.

He grabbed a piece of paper and a pen and began to work out a "pros" and "cons" list. Doing that — treating this like it was just a normal problem to be solved by some practical thinking — made him feel less nervous. Unfortunately, there seemed to be only two options, and the first had more "cons" than "pros."

The first option was to call social services. If they came around and saw the state of the house, they'd put a stop to the situation. They'd say it was no environment to bring up a child. A pig, maybe, but not a boy. Because downstairs, the house was looking more and more like a sty. The parrot was only out of its cage when Mom and Dad were in the living room, but that was all the time it needed to turn the place upside down. There were so many droppings scattered across the living room floor you had to watch your feet wherever you walked. The bird had torn at the furniture with its talons the same way it tore at its fruit at mealtimes. The chairs weren't just ripped now, all their stuffing had been yanked out and dragged across the floor. You'd think a chainsaw had been let loose in there, not just a parrot. There were even claw marks in the wallpaper, so deep it looked like a garden rake had scraped the walls.

But then the "cons" came thick and fast. Social services would be sure to take Ben away from the house and put him somewhere safe, and they'd probably prosecute his parents, too. But there was no way they'd blame the bird. They'd blame his mom and dad. And it wasn't their fault. He didn't know how, but he was sure that Igor was controlling both their minds. They were acting more like robots, programed to obey the bird's will, than people who knew what they were doing.

And the animal cruelty services would also be sure to have Rex sent back to the shelter, and that would be the last he'd ever see of his pet.

The only alternative was to play it by ear, and take each day as it came. To keep out of Igor's way as much as he could until he was old enough to leave home and get a place of his own, as far away as possible. The drawback? Ben was only twelve years old, and the day he could leave home was years and years away.

Until then, he thought, he could stay out of the house as much as possible, stay with friends and relatives whenever he could. His new-style zombie parents probably wouldn't even notice if he didn't come home that often. And though he was on vacation now, school started again in a week and he'd be there all day. He could join some of the clubs and try out for some sports teams. That might keep him out after school and on weekends. Maybe he could even find some sort of exchange scheme where you swapped places with a foreign student and spent a whole semester in another country.

But Ben didn't really want to leave his parents under Igor's spell. He didn't want to stay away from home at all. Why should that parrot be allowed to push him out?

He fell asleep thinking about it.

* * *

Ben slept soundly until a faint flapping of wings made him twitch and stir under the covers. He opened his eyes and shivered.

He'd never realized before just how many shadows there were in a dark bedroom. Towering dark blobs, each of them as black as parrots' eyes. A breathless tension hung over them as if there was an unseen monster in the darkness, holding its breath to remain hidden.

There was the shadow of the open closet door, shadows of half-closed drawers, shadows of clothes tossed on to the floor, and plenty of shadows where you couldn't tell quite what they were. But then he saw an unmistakable shadow.

Igor was perched at the end of the bed, with folded wings — a big, bulky, bird-shaped lump of black. The bird's low gurgling chuckle broke the darkness.

Cold sweat beaded on Ben's skin. The creature hopped down onto the bed and began to claw its way up the covers toward him.

Before Ben had fallen asleep, he'd thought his problem would be staying alive until he was old enough to leave home. Now his problem was staying alive long enough to see morning.

He needed to spring out of his bed, but he was paralyzed with fear. It was as if icy hands were holding him still. He couldn't scream. He felt as though he were being choked.

But Igor had no problem speaking. *"Time to die!"* it screamed.

The bird reached the part of the bed where Ben's body lay, and hopped on top, its talons biting into the flesh of his leg.

"Time to die!" it screeched in its high-pitched parrot voice.

The bird began clambering over Ben's body toward his face and head. The boy felt the jab of the claws again, as, with another hop, Igor reached his stomach. Then the claws were pressing so deeply into his chest that Ben expected blood to start seeping through the sheets. The bird's foul stink made him curl up his face. He tried to back away, but there was nowhere to go.

The black shadow of the bird's face parted, and Ben realized that it was opening its beak to attack. He knew that beak was sharper than razor blades. He'd watched it crack nuts with ease and had no doubt it could crack his bones just as easily.

Ben's hand fumbled around by his bed, trying to find something to ward off the bird. He found his alarm clock, but that was too small to do any damage. His fingers brushed the bedside lamp, but that was plugged into the wall socket. He switched on the lamp and shrank back into the pillow as brightness flooded Igor's face.

The bird's tongue looked like a dry, wriggling finger, pointing at him. Its huge eyes seemed somehow sharper, as black as newly laid tar. Its beak appeared to have spread into an evil grin, more jagged and savage than ever.

Its foul-smelling bird breath washed over Ben's face in a disgusting blast.

"Igor! There you are!"

It was Mom, standing in the open doorway. She was looking at the bed, but her gaze was completely vacant. She held her hand out, and Igor flew off the bed and landed on her wrist.

"I couldn't sleep so I was cleaning Igor's cage downstairs," she said, "and he flew across the room and into the hall. The door was shut, but he used his claws to turn the handle and get through. Isn't he clever? Then he found his way upstairs and to your room. He must have opened your door, too; it's as if he knew exactly where you were."

She stroked Igor's hideous gnarled head. "I'm glad to see you both getting along so well," she said. "Maybe we ought to move Igor *permanently* into your room."

"No!" Ben yelled. "I mean — it's not big enough. He needs more space."

"I suppose you're right," Mom said, a concerned look spreading across her face, "but perhaps we should think about giving him free run of the house. He obviously knows how to get around the place. And he can open all the doors with those claws of his."

Ben noticed his alarm clock on the bedside table. "Just a minute, Mom," he said. "It's only half-past six in the morning. Why are you cleaning his cage this early?"

"Oh, I was lying in bed all night feeling that I was being selfish by relaxing," she said.

Ben noticed how flesh-crawlingly unnatural her voice had become. It sounded more like a robot's voice, with a little space between each word.

"And I was just thinking *What can I do for Igor, what can*

I do for Igor?" she continued. "Then I realized. I could clean his cage again. I hadn't done it since last night. It's odd — it's almost as if Igor was calling me, in my mind — calling me downstairs to open his cage door." Then she turned and smiled. "Isn't he clever?"

She left the room with the bird on her shoulder, like some sort of zombie pirate, absentmindedly stroking its belly. Ben's mom was now completely under its spell, and it was very likely that his dad would be just the same.

Ben was totally alone.

Ben's heart was still racing five minutes later, his pulse pounding like tiny hammers against his temples. Then as he began to breathe regularly again, he realized that the chugging sound in his ears wasn't coming from his chest anymore. It seemed to be coming from the drawer of his bedside cabinet — a mechanical sound, not the frenzied beat of his heart.

Of course! It was the ticking of that huge, hideous pocket watch his grandfather had left him. He wished it was *all* his grandfather had ever left his family.

He pulled open the drawer, reached inside, and

pulled it out, wondering why his grandfather would ever have given him such a thing. He must have known Ben would own a digital watch, and that a relic like that belonged in a dusty, old museum, not some modern kid's pocket.

But he hadn't just left it to him in his will. He'd asked Ben's mom to pass it along as soon as possible, as if it was *important* for Ben to have it immediately.

Ben felt goose bumps prickling on his arms as something occurred to him. He remembered how he'd visited Grandpa's grave with Rex and had stood staring at the stone, thinking, *Only you know the truth about that bird, Grandpa, and there's no way you can tell me.*

But maybe that wasn't true. Maybe Grandpa *had* found a way to tell him. A way to warn him.

Maybe he had a very good reason for leaving Ben the watch.

It was such an odd present that Ben felt sure there was more to it than met the eye. Maybe some kind of clue about the parrot. Was that possible?

He examined the timepiece, front and back, looking for telltale markings.

There was an engraving on the back, but it was just a regular one.

TO EDWARD STEVENS
ON THE EVENT OF HIS BIRTHDAY
WITH LOVE FROM
MOTHER AND FATHER

Ben read and reread those words, looking for some kind of coded message, but they seemed straightforward enough.

He turned the watch around and studied the numbers on its face. They were Roman numerals, but that was common enough in old watches. Even their old grandfather clock downstairs had Roman numerals. He looked for any other kind of clue.

There was nothing.

Suddenly, Ben had another idea. Maybe the watch had some kind of message hidden in it. He examined the back and noticed that it had tiny little screws in it; he could unscrew them and have a look inside. Ben remembered that he had a set of miniature screwdrivers in one of his bedroom drawers. He sat with the watch in his lap, twiddling with the tiny screws, and accidentally jabbing himself in the hand with the screwdriver blade. Finally, he managed to pull off the back of the watch.

There was a piece of paper in there, folded up very small. Grandpa *had* used the watch to smuggle a message to him.

Ben opened it up very carefully. There was writing on both sides. One side had a message from Grandpa on it, handwritten in blue ink. The writing looked like the kind of graffiti a spider might make. It was all over the place, and the writing was tiny. Grandpa must have been in a great hurry when he wrote it.

Ben lay on the bed with the paper on the pillow and began to read:

Dear Ben,

If this message has reached you, then I will already be dead. I put the note in here as I knew that you would find it — you've always been a smart boy. Igor will be with you in your house and your parents will be trapped under his spell, just as I am. I fell and burned my hand on the fire, and it woke me from the parrot's control long enough to write you this note and to tell you what you can do to kill him.

The parrot is possessed by a demon, Ben. This demon will kill me very soon, and I will be powerless to stop it — but you still have a chance to save your parents.

I have ordered a book on driving out demons, but I doubt I'll have time to get it from the store. But you can pick it up! Just say it is for me —

Ben heard a noise outside the window, and his heart did a back flip. He'd heard a rustle of wings. And then — a beak rapping on the glass. He looked behind him with terror-filled eyes, dropping the paper. Then he breathed a sigh of relief, the breath shooting out of him like he'd been punched in the stomach. It was just a branch from the tree outside, brushing against his window in the breeze. He'd thought it had been the bird. The parrot that killed Grandpa.

He continued reading, his whole body now shaking.

. . . all you need to do is go and get it. The demon MUST be stopped, Ben. It moves into people's homes, has its fun with them, and then discards them — and they always die.

Each night, it cackles as it makes me listen to all the terrible things that it has done. It is driving me mad!

But it never tells stories about children that it has possessed and killed. I don't think that it can control them — and this is what makes you the only one who can get rid of it.

Your mom and dad won't believe what I've said — your mom was always far too level-headed — so it is down to you, Ben. Hurry!

Don't let it win. Get the book, Ben — and get rid of the demon.

Good luck.

Love, Grandpa

Ben turned the piece of paper over. It was a receipt for a book order. The book was titled *Driving Out Demons*. There was a scribbled date on it, and Ben realized that it would be in the store by now. The address showed that the bookstore was in Grandpa's town, which was a few miles away.

Ben took some time to plan his route. He printed out a map from a location finder site on the Internet showing him exactly how to find the street where the bookstore was. He wrote down which bus he would need and when it would arrive.

Just before he set off to find the store, he took a bowl of dog food outside to Rex in the shed. He noticed that weeds were beginning to poke out between the flowers, and that the grass was getting overgrown. Dad was no longer spending any time at all on the garden. It had previously been his pride and joy, the same as the living room had been Mom's.

Rex was in the shed, curled up on his sheets.

"Don't worry, boy," Ben said. "I'm off to get a book that'll show me how to stop Igor. And you were right from the start. It's not just a bird. There's a demon inside it. But not for long, boy. Not for long."

Rex just whimpered and stared at Ben.

"You'll be back in the house again soon, boy," Ben said. "I promise."

He could hear hammering. He guessed it was the nextdoor neighbors working on their house. But when he walked through the kitchen, into the hall and out through the front door, he saw his dad balancing halfway up a pair of ladders, fitting a huge set of metal bars to his and Mom's bedroom window. More sets of bars were leaning against the fence, waiting to be fastened to the other windows. So they hadn't *just* been out buying food and toys for Igor. They'd also been buying enough metal to build the *Titanic*.

"Dad, what are you doing?" Ben asked, alarmed.

His dad didn't seem to hear him and continued to work on the metal bars.

Ben shouted, trying to snap him out of his daze. "Dad, why are you putting up bars?"

"Igor wants it done," his dad replied. "We've given him free run of the house now, but he's really unhappy that we kept him in a cage for a few days. He said that we're all going to find out what it's like living behind bars. Once they're all done, we're going to be locked inside with Igor and he's going to punish us. We deserve it, though. Don't we, Ben?"

Ben began to back away.

"I've only got enough to finish all the front windows at the moment," his dad continued. "Tomorrow I'll go and get some more for the back windows and the doors. Then Igor will have what he wants."

Ben wasn't listening anymore. He was hurrying down the path and through the front gate. He only looked back once at the house, and when he did it looked like the beginnings of a giant cage.

Ben tried to make himself comfortable on the bus seat. Its cushion had been vandalized, with a great long strip torn out of it, but he had to admit, it still looked in pretty good shape compared with the chairs in his own living room. He looked out of the dusty window, watching the streets slide by as the bus entered the town in which his grandfather used to live.

He didn't much like taking buses on unfamiliar routes. It was always so hard to figure out exactly where to get off and it was so easy to miss your stop. He gripped his printouts from the Internet and kept a sharp eye out for the right stop.

He'd never liked the town. There were dirty apartment buildings looming over you wherever you walked, and the center was full of dust, dirt, and exhaust fumes.

Ben got off the bus and pulled the street map out of his pocket. It seemed easy enough to follow but when he reached the place where the street was supposed to be, on the far side of the town, he thought he must have done something wrong. It looked abandoned, with its rows of ancient warehouses standing side by side, quietly rotting away. Most of their windowpanes were broken, and there was a strange stillness in the street. But when he looked up at the rusty sign on the wall above him, it did say Brick Street. That was where Rare Books was. He was in the right place after all.

He didn't feel very safe being there alone and wished he had Rex at his heel, but he pushed on, following the building numbers.

He reached the spot where the bookstore was supposed to be and found himself looking over an iron railing. A set of crumbling concrete steps led to a dark basement. Was there really a store tucked away down there?

He hesitated at the top for a few moments, then, step by step, made his way down.

There *was* a store, looking like it was crouching under the alcove. It looked ancient — like it had been lurking underground for centuries and hadn't noticed the town being built above and around it. Its bricks were so dirty that Ben was sure they'd never seen water.

RARE BOOKS was written in faded gold paint on the banner above its window. It looked gloomy inside the dust-encrusted glass. He couldn't see anything much at all through it, but from what he could make out, it looked more like a cave than a bookstore.

He turned the door handle and pushed the door open. It creaked like a train screeching to a sudden halt. Dusty old books lined every wall, many of them overflowing from their bookcases. The smell of their leather bindings and slowly crumbling pages hit him like a slap in the face.

He'd never much liked secondhand bookstores. And *everything* about this store seemed creepy.

Much of the writing on the book spines was written in an old language of some kind — probably Latin, he thought — but even though he couldn't read it himself, he could tell that these weren't nice storybooks or fun reading for the beach. Some of the spines had snarling demons' heads painted below the titles, or magical symbols embedded into their gloomy bindings.

Ben made his way slowly through the aisles. They were like a maze, twisting and turning toward a large, old counter. At first, it looked more like another stack of books, but he could see a bobbing head behind the towering piles.

"Hello?" Ben ventured.

An old man emerged from behind a stack of ancient books. He was bald, with a finely trimmed, graying goatee. From the look of his clothes, it seemed as though the man was stuck in a time warp. He gave Ben a sharp, suspicious look.

"A boy?" he snapped. "Don't you know what kind of store this is? Not suitable for children! Go away!"

Ben said nothing and handed over the book receipt.

The man snatched it off him and looked at it, squinting. "Ah, *Driving Out Demons*," he said. "Yes, all right, then. This little volume came in last week. I had to order it from abroad, you know. Are you picking it up for Mr. Stevens?"

"Sort of," Ben said, peering at the pendants hanging around the old guy's neck. They had weird symbols on them, and Ben wondered if they were for protection.

"Yes, yes, a charming man. Seemed terribly worried, though, when he was here. He was having some kind of trouble with a possessed . . . now what was it? Some sort of bird, I think. A cockatoo, was it?"

"A parrot," Ben corrected.

"Ah, yes — I remember now. He told me about it. I recommended this book to him. Very rare, you know. Set him back two hundred dollars. But it works, and that's what's important. Now, where did I put it?"

He lifted a box of books onto the table and began rummaging through it. "And how *is* Mr. Stevens?" he said as his fingers, which were as thin as bones, flicked and clicked through the spines.

"Dead," Ben said, suddenly feeling sad. "The parrot killed him."

The old man gave Ben a sorry look. "How unfortunate," he murmured, "but so often the way. You have to act very fast indeed if one of your pets is possessed by a demon. I'm afraid I won't be able to give you his money back, though, my boy. The book has already been shipped so you must take it with you."

"I want to," Ben said. "The bird is in my house now."

"My word!" the bookseller said. "Then you really do need the book."

"Can *you* help me at all?" Ben asked. "Do you know anything about demons?"

"A little," the bookseller said, pausing from his search for a moment. "I've encountered a few in my time. There are several types, you know. The one that's troubling you is probably a terrestrial demon — one that's been cast out of the spirit world and has to dwell here on Earth with us humans. They usually dwell in tombs, mountains, or other abandoned, lonely places, but some are a little braver, I'm afraid."

"And they can really possess birds?" Ben asked, hugely relieved that someone else was taking this seriously.

"Yes, indeed. They can take over their bodies and speak through their mouths. Has this parrot been saying nasty things?"

Ben nodded.

"Yes, that's to be expected. Well, at least the one you've got is the weakest kind of demon, so there's hope. It's only the lesser demons who inhabit other bodies. They don't have the skill to create a body of their own, you see. Luckily, they aren't strong enough to possess human beings, but they do have the ability to control adult human subjects."

"So it isn't that dangerous?" Ben asked.

"Not that dangerous? Oh, make no mistake, it's a killer. A very nasty, vicious demon indeed — deadlier than a nest of vipers." The man pulled out a thin, leather-bound volume. "Ah! Here's your book."

For a book that small to have cost two hundred dollars, Ben reckoned, it had to contain some very valuable information.

The storekeeper opened it to a chapter of instructions. "This will tell you everything you have to say to get rid of it," he said. "Can you contain the bird while you do it?"

"Contain it?" Ben asked.

"Yes. It'll put up quite a struggle." The storekeeper turned the page. "Where does it sleep?"

Ben thought for a moment. "In its cage, I *think*."

"That sounds likely. It'll be the bird's natural instincts taking over. It'll want to rest on the perch. So that's good. If you can manage to lock it inside the cage while you perform the ritual, it'll have much less chance of, well, killing you."

"Killing me?" Ben swallowed hard.

"Yes. You know, tearing your throat out, plucking

your heart from your chest with its beak and claws . . . that sort of thing." The old man moved about behind the counter, shifting dusty volumes this way and that. "It *will* put up a fight, though. In fact, it'll do everything it possibly can to finish you off. So be very careful."

"But if I do it properly," Ben said, trying to organize his thoughts, "and say all the words right, will the demon be dead?"

"Dead? I'm afraid not, young man! Demons are immortal, so you can't actually kill them. But you will drive it out of the parrot's body and send it shooting a good long way away from your house. It'll never find its way back. It'll end up somewhere on the other side of the world, probably. Then it'll find another creature's body to possess. Hopefully, it'll end up inside something harmless like a snail or a fish."

He handed over the book and Ben noticed an instruction, written in capital letters on the first page: BE SURE TO PRONOUNCE EVERY WORD EXACTLY AS WRITTEN.

"Thanks," said Ben.

"Good luck," the bookseller said. "Believe me, my boy, you'll need it!"

When he arrived home, the house was looking even more like a birdcage. He noticed a couple of neighbors staring over their fence at the metal bars his dad had attached to the window. Tomorrow, Dad would be going out to buy more. Bars to attach to the back windows and the doors. Then they'd all be locked inside with Igor. He dreaded to think what Igor's punishment would be like. He knew he had to get rid of the bird that night, so he'd never have to find out.

Until then, he had to keep the book safely hidden. He thought that slipping it under his mattress would be his best bet, since Mom hadn't hassled him about making his bed for days.

Ben entered the house. His parents were in the living room, talking to Igor behind the closed door. Ben hurried upstairs. Once he was in his room, he'd be able to barricade the door.

But when he reached his room, he found the door wide open, the covers pulled off his bed, and the mattress ripped and torn, its stuffing and springs all poking out. Igor had visited again.

Igor certainly didn't want Ben to have another comfortable night's sleep. Or maybe the hideous creature was demonstrating what it intended to do to him.

Ben's eyes swept across the room. It wasn't just the bed that had been damaged. His things were all thrown off his desk, and his computer screen had been scored by sharp talons.

The closet door was flung open, and Ben looked inside. All his clothes hung in tatters from their hangers. He ran his fingers through the dangling rags, knowing that the final showdown with Igor was just a few hours away.

Ben entered the living room quietly and locked the door behind him. As softly as he could, Ben dragged his mom's favorite bookshelf across the door, barricading himself in with Igor. The room was dark, and the parrot cage was lost in the pool of shadows at the far end. With the light off, he wouldn't be able to see to lock it up.

His hand on the switch, something occurred to Ben.

Igor might not be in the cage at all. The door might not have been properly locked, and Igor might be loose in the room! Perhaps the old parrot was perched silently just an arm's length away, hidden in one of the shadows!

Ben forced himself to calm down.

He was about to find out.

It's now or never, he thought, and switched on the light.

The room lit up instantly. He jolted to see two eyes staring right at him. But he was just seeing his own eyes reflecting back from the wall mirror. The *broken* wall mirror. It was shattered, and shards of broken glass lay across the carpet. But at least the bird wasn't loose. In fact, an expensive-looking cover of crushed red velvet had been placed over its cage to help it sleep. The deep red cover had molded itself to fit every corner and curve on the cage so well that Ben wondered if his parents had actually had it custom-made.

The good thing was: Igor was underneath it and wouldn't even know that the light was on, or that Ben was in the room. That cover would blot out all light.

But Ben would have to raise it to lock the cage door.

And it was the only thing stopping Igor from breaking free.

He gently placed the spell book on the once luxurious sofa and crept across the room.

He paused by the cage.

What if Igor's awake in there? he thought. *Do demons sleep?*

He shuddered at the thought of Igor perching in there, wide awake, just waiting for him to pull up the cover so it could shoot out of the cage and at him.

He began to pull it slowly upward, his hand quivering as it tugged.

Up slid the cover . . . and off.

Igor was asleep — but Ben nearly gasped aloud at the *way* it was sleeping. The parrot was hanging upside down like a bat, clutching tightly to the perch with its claws.

Ben knew he had no time to gape. He had to move fast. His hand shot to the cage door, slammed it shut, and slid the little bolt into place.

As he did it, Igor woke up.

"Sorry to disturb your sleep," Ben said, his confidence growing now that he knew the cage was bolted.

The parrot hopped onto its perch, eyeing him. *"Ready to die?"* it said quietly. Ben shivered, as if a pair of icy bird talons had clamped down on his shoulders. Igor didn't look worried at all.

Until he saw the book.

As soon as Ben picked up *Driving Out Demons* from the sofa, the creature seemed a little unsettled. It croaked curiously and craned its head against the bars as if trying to see the book better.

"This is the end," Ben said, looking into the parrot's eyes at the demon lurking inside its body. "I don't know how you got inside that bird, but you're about to leave. I'm sending you hundreds of miles away, so you'll end up possessing some creature at the bottom of a lake in the middle of nowhere. Then you won't be able to hurt anyone else."

The bird cocked its head. *"Open the cage,"* it said, sounding less confident now.

"Not on your life," Ben replied.

"Open the cage!" Igor screeched. The bird rattled the bars with its claws and bashed its ancient head against the metal frame. *"Open the cage, open the cage, open the cage!"*

But all Ben opened was the book. He reread the

instruction at the top: BE SURE TO PRONOUNCE EVERY WORD EXACTLY AS WRITTEN.

That would be difficult. The words didn't look like any language he knew. He'd really have to focus on getting it right.

Igor's voice began to croak again, although this time it sounded much less threatening. "*Open the cage, and we can be friends. Open the cage, and I can give you anything. Open the cage, and I can protect you. Open the cage, and I can kill your enemies.*"

But Ben knew that the demon was scared.

"*OPEN THE CAGE!*" it screamed.

Ben started to read aloud from the page, taking it slowly, the syllables of the strange speech tumbling clumsily over his tongue. Igor paced nervously up and down the perch as he spoke.

As Ben finished the first line, his mom's potpourri dish flew off the mantelpiece and cracked him in the back of the head. Luckily, it was only plastic and did no serious damage, but it had dumped its dung and mess on him. The bird was using its powers to affect things in the room, but Ben knew he had to continue reading without hesitation, no matter how bad it got.

He heard a scraping noise. A couple of old videotapes had begun to slide across the floor from the side of the TV. They'd be much heavier than a little potpourri dish.

They flew through the air, aiming at his head. He ducked and they flew past, one of them bouncing against the cage bars. Now Ben knew how the room had become such a mess. He'd wondered how a bird's wings could be strong enough to pick up furniture and hurl it across a room. But now he knew that Igor didn't need to pick up anything. The demon lurking inside the bird had the power to move things with its mind. And now it was using those powers to their full extent.

The newspapers from the table hurled themselves at him next, *whap, whap, whap,* against his back. Then more of the dung and sawdust flew up from the floor, as if an angry tornado was hurling it at his face and head, rubbing it in his hair, pushing it in his ears, and aiming it at his mouth to stop him from reading. He spat as something horrible brushed his lips. He'd mispronounced a word thanks to that attack. But there was no time to go back, so he covered his mouth as best he could with his free hand and continued reading.

As Ben got halfway down the page, Igor started to go crazy, throwing itself against the bars so hard that Ben almost thought it might break through them. Again and again it hurled itself, screaming out threats as it did.

The furniture started to slide across the room. The desk turned itself over and landed with a loud crash. A vase hurled itself at him and smashed against the wall. Then, worst of all, the main lightbulb overhead blew, exploding like a gunshot and plunging the room into darkness. Ben could no longer see the page. He could no longer continue reading.

The bird cackled with glee, but Ben had planned well. He pulled the flashlight out of his pocket, clicked it on, and let the beam find the next line of text.

As he continued to read, the bird became increasingly furious, clanging its beak against the bars and rocking the cage back and forth as if trying to tip it over. Its talons tore at the cage door, but the bolt remained firmly in place. Another heavy table lamp flew through the air, and Ben only just managed to duck out of the way in time. It smashed through the living room window. Ben felt the cold night air rush in.

Then he heard commotion from upstairs. His parents had woken up. They were hurrying downstairs. Ben could hear his mother on the other side of the door screaming, "Igor! Are you all right? Igor?"

It was good that he'd locked the living room door. It was a strong mortise lock with a thick steel bolt. It would take them some time to break through it. More worryingly, Igor might break out of his own cage much more quickly. The demon had stopped using its powers to hurl tables and chairs around like they were Frisbees and was now focusing on something else instead.

It was starting to bend the cage bars apart!

The metal of the cage was turning as soft as silly putty — as soft as Ben's *insides* were starting to feel, as everything within him went loose with fear. He had to finish the spell fast.

He reached the final line, reading it even louder and bolder than the others, above the thudding of wings against metal, at the very top of his voice. The creature put up one final struggle, letting out a loud bellow and spitting flame as it clawed the air with its talons, then it finally crashed off the perch and hit the bottom of the cage, its head hanging limply to one side.

When Ben finished, he felt something invisible whisk out of the bird, across the room, and through the shattered window.

Ben had done it. He'd driven out the demon!

He aimed the flashlight at the cage and shuddered as the parrot's body began to crumple in on itself. Parts of it began to explode like pus-filled pimples, splattering the inside of the cage. Then the parrot collapsed into an oozing mass of dead flesh on the cage bottom, still spitting and bubbling as if it was being roasted for a revolting meal. Ben edged closer as the mass continued to cackle and sizzle, finally sinking into a disgusting pool. It looked like the parrot's body had been dead for many years, and only the demon inhabiting it had kept it animated.

There was a thumping on the living room door.

Ben could hear Dad shouting. "What's going on in there?"

Ben staggered through the debris and unlocked the door.

Light flooded in from the kitchen as his dad and mom burst into the living room. They appeared to be back to normal. They no longer had that dazed look in their eyes. A woken-up-from-sleep-and-still-slightly-dozy look, certainly, but not that chilling zombie stare. And when Mom spoke, she no longer sounded like a robot, but like she always used to sound.

"What happened to the light?" she asked.

But Dad didn't need the light to tell that the room had been completely trashed. The moon was bright outside and its silver glow shone in, highlighting the jagged shards of glass framing the broken window. He saw the debris littering the floor and all the destroyed furniture. "What happened here?" he demanded angrily. It was as if he'd never seen the living room like this before.

Ben had to think fast. "I just came down for a snack," he said, "and some burglars had broken into the living room. Or maybe they were just hooligans. They were trashing the place. I came in and scared them off."

"Where's that old bird of Grandpa's?" Dad said.

"I think it must have gotten loose and flown away," Ben said.

"Well, at least one good thing came out of this,

then, if it's gone," Dad said. "Whose idea was it to keep the awful creature in the *living room* in the first place?"

"Not mine," Mom said. "I hated it at first sight."

Ben smiled as Mom held him tight. Things were *definitely* getting back to normal.

"Let's get into the light," Mom said, and she and Ben walked into the kitchen.

He caught a glimpse of himself in the hallway mirror: bruised, scratched, and covered in sawdust and parrot droppings.

"Would you like some hot chocolate?" Mom asked.

Ben nodded and sat down on a kitchen chair as his mom put the kettle on the stove.

"I'll go and call the police," she said.

Ben watched her hurry to the hallway, closing the door behind her.

"And I'll go and check if they've taken anything," Dad added, ruffling Ben's hair and walking out of the room.

Ben sat for a moment, and smiled, enjoying the normality that had once again entered his life. Then, above the rumbling sound of the kettle, Ben heard a scratching against the back door.

Rex! he smiled to himself, hurrying to the back door.

He removed the chain, twisted the key, and pulled it open. Rex slunk back inside.

"Welcome back, boy!" Ben said.

Now things really *were* back to normal. The demon had gone, and his dog was happy to return and share the house with him. All the damage would be repaired in time. His parents would buy new wallpaper and a new bed for him, and he'd replace the clothes in his closet one by one. Within a few months, it would be like nothing bad had ever happened at all.

Except . . .

Somehow Rex looked different. The fur on his back was rising.

"What's up, Rex?" Ben said. "The demon's gone now. There's nothing bad in the house. Not anymore."

Ben looked at the big dog. Why was Rex growling? From the hall, he could still hear his mom on the phone with the police.

Ben reached a hand out to stroke Rex, but something in him made him pull it back instinctively.

Why did I do that? he thought.

Because you want to keep the hand, that's why, Ben's brain answered in a flash.

Then it dawned on him. There *was* something different about Rex. The dog looked *mean* and was glaring at him like it had murder on its mind.

"Mom," he called out nervously, but his fear seemed to trap his voice in his throat.

Ben reached a foot down to the floor, but Rex growled so fiercely that he froze like a statue, then promptly returned to his seat and sat there as if glued to it. A nightmare thought had struck him.

What if I read the banishing spell incorrectly? Ben thought as sweat began to bead on his neck. Could that mistake have prevented it from working properly? Could it be that instead of flinging the demon hundreds of miles away to look for a new animal body to possess, it had simply traveled a short distance?

Like into *his own yard?*

The growling grew louder, and Ben shook with fear. He saw Rex rise up to his full height. Saw the huge dog's top lip curled back to reveal glistening white teeth.

In that moment, Ben asked himself a question. *What would be much worse than sharing a house with a parrot possessed by a vicious demon?*

The answer came to him in a heartbeat. *Sharing a house with a big dog possessed by a vicious demon.*

Rex began to growl more loudly. A deep, nasty growl, which made every muscle in Ben's body tense up, and every pore in his skin tingle and shimmer with cold sweat.

And the growl shaped itself into terrible, guttural words.

"I killed your grandpa."

Laura was late.

Usually, she was as punctual as the Swiss clock on the living room mantelpiece, arriving at seven o'clock on the dot.

But tonight was different. It was twenty past seven and she still hadn't arrived. Laura was their babysitter — though Jessica and her brother, Robbie, at eleven and ten years old, were hardly babies anymore. Even their little sister, Megan, was four years old now, so Jessica thought that a new word needed to be invented. Anything but *baby*sitter. That was just plain embarrassing.

Jessica just wished Laura would hurry up, then Mom and Dad could stop complaining and leave for their wedding anniversary dinner in town. Dad was fidgeting like he had fleas, and Mom was dialing and redialing Laura's cell phone, but each time she did, she was put through to voice mail.

"Why has she turned off her phone?" Mom groaned. "She must know we'd be calling her."

"This isn't like Laura," Dad said. "It's not like her at all."

Jessica thought that her parents should just leave *her* in charge. She knew she was perfectly capable of looking after her brother and sister by herself, and it would have been great having the power to send Robbie to bed.

But Jessica had to admit, having Laura look after them was the next best thing to letting them look after themselves, anyway. She was really cool, and though she was strict about things like bedtimes and eating too much junk food, they could do pretty much whatever they wanted when she was in charge.

"Maybe it's about time we got a new babysitter," Mom said impatiently.

That made Jessica frown. Someone else might not be as nice as Laura. "I'm sure it's not her fault," she piped up. "Maybe there's been an emergency."

"There *is* an emergency," Dad said, pacing the floor now like a caged lion. "We're late for dinner."

"Jess, could you just go upstairs and look out the window before your dad wears a hole in the new carpet?" Mom said. "You'll be able to see her coming down the street."

Jessica nodded. She was glad to get out of the room. There was so much tension in there that you could feel it in the air.

There was a switch in the hall to turn on the landing light, but she didn't bother with it as she ran upstairs.

She was just reaching out with her foot to the top step when it happened.

A hideous creature with long green fingernails, pointed ears, a chalk-white face, and a bloodstained mouth sprang out of the shadows, hissing at her like a snake and clawing at Jessica's chest.

Jessica shrieked, lost her footing, and slipped, skidding as if the stairs were made of ice. She almost tumbled all the way back down.

"What is it?" Dad called up the stairs. "What's wrong?"

Jessica gripped the banister rail to balance herself and looked up again. This time, she realized that the creature was Megan. Her little sister was grinning through her ghoulish makeup. Jessica ran a finger across Megan's face. The white came off on its tip. "Just another one of Robbie's stupid makeup experiments," Jessica shouted back downstairs. "And this time I nearly broke my leg!"

She hadn't broken her leg, but she *had* given her ankle a nasty twist. Jessica bet it would swell up like a water-filled balloon and turn as purple as a bunch of grapes. And her school had an important basketball game coming up at the end of the week. Jessica was one of the best on the team and loved playing, but now she might have to sit the whole thing out, watching from the side. *Stupid, stupid Robbie!*

"Scaredy-cat, scaredy-cat, Jessie is a scaredy-cat!" Megan piped up.

Robbie stood in his bedroom doorway, a big grin spreading across his face. "Not bad, eh?" he said. "She's supposed to be a little ghoul. Much more interesting than a little *girl*, don't you think?"

"You'll need makeup *yourself* after I've finished with you, Robbie — to cover up your bruises!" Jessica shouted at her brother.

Robbie's ambition was to be a makeup artist for horror films. He was always saying that when he was older he would go to Hollywood to create monsters for films. Jessica wished he'd hurry up and get going, then she'd finally have some peace.

He was always practicing his horror makeup and had lots of books with pictures of monsters in them that he used to get his ideas. Mostly he practiced on Megan. A few times, he'd painted wounds on her arms and legs that looked so realistic Mom had almost called an ambulance. But usually, he just turned their sweet, pretty, little four-year-old sister into some kind of horrible supernatural creature.

"You'd better get that makeup off Megan before Laura arrives," Jessica told him.

"Aw, why?" Robbie said. "It's fun to frighten Laura, too. We could have Megan crouch down behind the sofa and leap out when she comes through the —"

"You shouldn't be using Megan for that kind of thing," Jessica snapped. "You'll give her nightmares."

"I could turn *you* into a monster instead, Jess," Robbie suggested. "It wouldn't take long. You've got such a head start. . . ."

But when he saw that Jessica wasn't laughing, he gave in. "All right, all right," he said, taking Megan by the hand and leading her back to his room to wipe off the makeup.

"I *like* the makeup!" Megan insisted as Robbie led her away. "I like looking scary!"

Jessica smiled, in spite of herself. Megan and Robbie, though annoying on occasion, were always full of surprises.

She followed them into Robbie's room. It was like walking into the Chamber of Horrors section of a waxworks museum. There were werewolf and Frankenstein monster masks along the walls; vampire, ghoul, and zombie models along the shelves; and books about every kind of hideous supernatural creature imaginable. Unlike most of his friends, Robbie wasn't into modern horror films. He preferred the classic old black-and-white ones that he recorded off the TV: *The Creature from the Black Lagoon*, *The Mummy*, *The Monster That Challenged the World*, *The Ghost of Frankenstein*, *Son of*

Dracula. Stacks and stacks of videotapes towered up from the floor.

Jessica remembered why she had come upstairs, and she headed, limping, toward her own room to look through the window for any sign of Laura. Her ankle was really sore.

She had just made it over to the window when the shrill *briiiiing* of the doorbell stopped her in her tracks. *Better late than never*, she thought.

She began to limp back downstairs, taking the steps carefully as her ankle continued to throb.

Her parents were letting Laura in.

"Sorry I'm late," Laura was saying.

Jessica noticed that the babysitter's voice sounded a little flatter and deeper than usual, as if she had a cold. She looked unwell, too. Normally her cheeks were as rosy as red apples, but tonight her face was pale. And Jessica saw that she was panting, out of breath. *She must have run all the way here*, Jessica thought. She wondered what could have delayed Laura so.

"You might have called to let us know, Laura," Mom said sharply.

Laura began to speak again, but Dad had no time for

explanations. "Never mind now, let's just get going," he interrupted, "or we'll lose our reservation."

He and Mom turned and shouted, "See you later!" to Jessica, Robbie, and Megan, and then they bustled out into the dark.

Jessica reached the bottom of the stairs and stood with Laura to wave at Mom and Dad. "I never thought *you'd* be so late, Laura," she said with a teasing smile, as she watched Mom and Dad hurry down the front drive and get into the car.

Laura didn't return the smile. Instead she threw Jessica a dark glare.

Jessica stared at Laura in surprise. "I was only joking, Laura," she said. It wasn't like Laura to be moody. *Perhaps she really isn't feeling well, or has had a really bad day*, Jessica thought.

Waving to them, Mom and Dad drove down the street.

Laura shut the front door and decisively clicked the lock, applied the chain, and closed the door's thick curtain.

Jessica decided to make an effort to get back on Laura's good side by offering to make her a cup of coffee. But the words turned to dust in her mouth as Laura took off her coat and Jessica saw tiny speckles of red on her shirt. "Laura, you've got something on you," she muttered awkwardly.

Laura looked down at herself. "I cut myself earlier," she said coolly. "It was nothing. Forget it." But she made a halfhearted attempt at covering the stains with her jacket.

"Oh . . . OK . . ." Jessica said quietly. But it looked to her like Laura had been in some kind of a struggle. It wasn't just the red spots on her shirt, but the way the rest of her clothes were ruffled, and how her hair — normally perfectly in place — was messy, too. And wasn't that a bruise on her right arm? Jessica wondered if Laura had been in some kind of fight that she didn't want to talk about. Maybe that was why she was late.

Suddenly, Jessica was distracted by a rush of movement and noise as Robbie and Megan came cannoning down the stairs.

"Hiya, Laura!" they both shouted.

Laura, normally so chatty, replied with a curt nod.

Robbie didn't seem to notice and threw her a piece of candy. "Here — have a mint!" he shouted.

This was a regular routine. Laura was absolutely horrible at catching, so Robbie loved throwing things to her, just to watch her drop them. One of his favorite lines was: *Laura, you couldn't even catch a cold!*

But tonight, Laura's hand shot up in the air like a baseball player catching a fastball, her fingers snatching the candy in mid-flight.

Wow . . . Jessica breathed to herself. She met Robbie's gaze. He looked as startled as she felt.

Megan's mouth hung open with disbelief. "That was fantastic!" she said, breaking into a huge grin.

But Laura just shrugged.

Jessica decided to try to cheer up Laura again. Laura loved MTV, and Jessica watched it with her whenever Laura came to babysit. "Our favorite music show's about to begin, Laura," she said brightly. "Should I put it on?"

"No!" Laura snapped.

Robbie pushed forward, past Jess. "Way to go, Laura!" he said. "Jess watches far too much of that boy-band garbage as it is."

Jessica made a face at Robbie. He hated MTV. He just listened to film soundtracks. *Horror* film soundtracks, mainly. He said that the boy bands all sounded the same, but they didn't to Jessica.

Robbie made a face back, and then turned to Laura to continue his routine. "I know you're supposed to make us a meal tonight, Laura," he said, "but can I just have potato chips and chocolate? It'll save you from cooking, and I'm sure that Mom and Dad wouldn't mind."

"Yes, all right," Laura said. "Whatever."

Jessica couldn't believe it. Robbie always tried the "potato chips and chocolate" ploy with Laura. It was another of his standing jokes. Laura would always grin and say no — and sometimes give him a long lecture on healthy eating, too — to which he'd pretend to fall asleep. She'd *never* agreed to Robbie's suggestion before.

And looking at his incredulous beaming face, Jessica saw that Robbie couldn't believe Laura had agreed this time, either. "Great!" he said, hurrying off into the kitchen before Laura could change her mind.

Megan looked up at their babysitter, a thoughtful look on her face. "Where's Laura?" she asked innocently.

Laura just frowned at Megan, and then pushed past her into the living room.

Jessica stared down at her little sister. Was she making a joke? "Megan," she said, "what do you mean?"

Megan shrugged. "Usually Laura takes care of us, right," she said. And then she turned and scampered off to the kitchen, no doubt to ask Robbie to share his "dinner."

Sighing, Jessica followed, wincing as a spike of pain shot through her injured ankle. Had Megan realized something they hadn't? Jessica had suspected that *something* was wrong with Laura — but Megan seemed to think that the babysitter wasn't Laura at all. That it was somebody else. A stranger. In their house.

But, no, that was silly. Of course it was Laura. She was just in a bad mood. Maybe she'd had an argument with her boyfriend. Maybe she was stressed about her college work. Everyone had off-days, and this was one of Laura's.

Walking to the kitchen, Jessica stepped on a dropped mint. As she shook it off her sock, something else occurred to her.

Here — have a mint!

When Robbie had thrown Laura a mint, not only had she amazed them all by catching it, she had used her *left* hand to snatch the candy from the air. And Laura was right-handed. Jessica was pretty sure about that. They'd often sat playing videogames, and Laura always held the joystick in her right hand. And sometimes she'd sit in a chair writing letters or filling in her diary, and Jessica was *sure* that she'd always held the pen in her right hand, too.

Jessica felt a trembling in her stomach like the rush of tiny wings. "Robbie?" she said.

He was tearing open a large package of chips. "What?" he replied, offering the bag to Megan, who took a handful and then ran off toward the living room, her other hand crammed with chocolate cookies.

"Have you noticed anything weird about Laura?" Jessica asked.

"Do you want a list?" Robbie joked.

"No." Jessica sighed. "I mean weirder than *usual*. I mean, look at *you*. Laura always follows Mom and Dad's rules, but she just let you have all that . . ." she pointed to the chips and the bars of chocolate that Robbie had spread across the table, ". . . junk food instead of dinner."

"That is pretty weird, I suppose," Robbie agreed.

"And when she caught your mint, she used her left hand. But I'm pretty sure she isn't left-handed. She's right-handed."

"I've never noticed," Robbie said, sounding unconcerned. "It might just have been the nearest hand. Her other one might have been in her pocket. Or unbuttoning her jacket. Or picking her nose. Or maybe she's — what's that word? Ambiguous."

"Not *ambiguous*," Jessica said. "You mean *ambidextrous*. Someone who can use *both* hands. But I don't think Laura can."

"So what are you saying?" Robbie asked, spitting out some chips.

Jessica wasn't sure if Robbie could even hear her above the munching sound coming from his mouth, and wondered if it was worth continuing. "Nothing," she said, sighing. "But . . . Megan just asked her . . ."

Robbie raised his eyebrows. "Asked her what?"

"Where Laura was," Jessica replied.

"Really?" Robbie said, suddenly interested. "Are you sure?"

Jessica nodded. "Yes. But I mean, she's only four. . . ."

"Yes, but they say that you can't fool little kids the

way you can older ones and grown-ups," Robbie replied. "When weird things happen, they're supposed to be more aware of that stuff than we are."

"*Who* says?" Jessica asked curiously.

"I read it in one of my books," Robbie told her. "Like, if a house gets haunted, the tiniest kids usually see the ghosts first." He swallowed the last of the chips. "Why don't you go and keep an eye on Laura — watch for any other weird signs. I'll get some more food and join you in a minute."

"OK," Jessica agreed.

She limped into the living room. Her ankle was swelling up just as she'd feared. Normally, she'd expect Laura to be sympathetic. Tonight, there seemed no point in even mentioning it.

The babysitter was sitting stiffly upright in the chair at the far corner of the room. She'd switched off the tall lamp that stood next to it. She looked creepy sitting there in the shadows, her face blacked out by the gloom. She could have been one of the creatures in Robbie's books and films.

Jessica went and sat on the floor in front of the TV. She picked up the remote control from the carpet.

With a press of her index finger, the TV flickered to life.

The TV was tuned into MTV. One of her favorite music videos was playing. Jessica turned up the volume.

Laura leaped out of her chair like someone had set off a stick of dynamite beneath it. She clamped her hands over her ears. "TURN . . . IT . . . OFF!" Laura shrieked.

Jessica was so shocked by Laura's outburst that her fingers fumbled with the remote control and dropped it back on to the carpet.

Now Laura was really screaming. "TURN IT OFF — NOW!"

With shaking fingers, Jessica grabbed the remote and pressed the OFF button. The TV fell silent.

"Don't put that television on again," Laura snarled, glaring at Jessica. She looked almost seasick. Her green eyes seemed to pin Jessica to the spot. They were so intense that Jessica half expected a laser to blast out of them and blow her head off.

Green eyes?

Was that a trick of the light?

It didn't seem to be. Jessica felt the trembling in her stomach again.

Laura had *brown* eyes, not green.

Megan crept over to Jessica. "Laura wouldn't have done that," she whispered. "Why can't we have *Laura* back?"

The babysitter glared at them both and then stormed out of the room.

A moment later, Robbie came into the living room. "What's been going on?" he asked. "Laura looked greener than a golf course when I passed her in the hall!"

Jessica beckoned him over. "Sit here and talk to me," she whispered. "Let's look like we're playing video-games. The noise will drown us out so she won't be able to hear what we're saying if she tries to listen."

Robbie nodded and Jessica switched on the game.

"All I did was switch on MTV," Jessica began. "One of my favorite songs came on — and I know Laura likes it, too — last week she told me she'd bought the CD. But tonight she hated it. It seemed to make her blood boil."

"If it was one of your boy bands, I know how she feels," Robbie joked.

Jessica gave him a shove. "The music really seemed to drive her crazy, though. She looked like she was going to pass out. And that's not all. Her eyes are different, too."

"Her eyes? How?" Robbie asked.

"They're green," Jessica replied. "Aren't they normally brown?"

"I don't remember, Jess," Robbie said, sighing dramatically. "I've never really looked. Are you sure?"

"*Totally* sure," Jessica replied firmly.

Robbie fell silent. And then slowly he said, "I think I might know what's going on."

Jessica leaned forward, eager to hear. But she and Robbie were jerked out of their conversation by the sound of shouting.

Following her brother's lead, Jessica limped as fast as she could into the hallway, to find the babysitter yelling at Megan. Their little sister was standing there, wide-eyed and white-faced with fear, her bottom lip trembling.

Jessica realized guiltily that she and Robbie had been so wrapped up in their conversation that they hadn't noticed Megan leave the room.

"*What* do you think you were doing, looking in my bag?" Laura shouted.

Jessica noticed Laura's bag, lying open on the floor.

"Don't you *dare* touch my things!" the babysitter said. "If you *ever* dare touch my things again —"

"But, Laura," Jessica interrupted, "you know how Megan loves to look at your sketchbook — and usually you ask her to get it out of your bag herself. . . ."

Robbie bent down to comfort Megan.

But the babysitter wasn't happy about being interrupted. "You two can just get back in there and keep quiet!" she shouted, roughly grabbing Robbie and Jessica by the arms and marching them back into the living room.

Inside, the videogame was still blasting away.

"More noise!" Laura shrieked angrily. She marched over and ripped the joysticks out of the console, threw them on to the floor, and then stomped on them repeatedly.

"Hey!" Robbie said angrily.

"Just wait till Dad hears about what you did," Jessica added.

But Laura kept stomping until both joysticks were shattered, with shards of plastic tangled into the carpet. "Now sit down and shut up," she said menacingly.

Out of the corner of her eye, Jessica saw that Megan had followed them in.

The babysitter grabbed Megan's hand. "And as for you . . ." she said, jerking Megan off her feet, ". . . bedtime."

"I don't like you as much as the real Laura," Megan said in a wavering voice.

Jessica and Robbie looked at each other, and then back at Megan, who was now being pulled, white-faced, out of the room in the babysitter's grip.

Normally, Megan threw a major fit when it was time for her to go to bed. She hated missing out on the fun that Jessica, Robbie, and Laura usually had together. Normally, she cried and shouted all the way upstairs and for the half hour it took her to fall asleep.

But tonight wasn't normal. Megan was utterly quiet.

"She's not even blubbering," Robbie said.

"That's because she's scared stiff," Jessica whispered. "You said you thought you knew what was going on," she added. "Hurry up and tell me. Do you think that a horrible twin sister of Laura's has taken her place, or something? Is that what it is?"

"It's worse than that," Robbie said seriously. "I think

our babysitter . . . is a doppelgänger. Laura's doppelgänger."

"A doppelgänger? What on Earth is that?" Jessica asked, confused.

"It's kind of like an opposite version of a person," Robbie told her. "I read about it in one of my books. A very nice person will have an evil doppelgänger, and vice versa. We all have one. And you can usually tell them apart because they're not *completely* identical. There might be small clues, like different color eyes, or slightly different teeth, or anything really — but stuff you'd have to be really eagle-eyed to notice."

"That's ridiculous!" Jessica exclaimed. "Are you saying we all have evil identical twins wandering around the world? How come we don't run into them all the time?"

"No, they're not in *our* world," Robbie replied. "Not exactly. They live in a parallel dimension, exactly the opposite of ours — everything nice in our world is horrible in theirs, everything right is wrong, everything good is evil. All they want is to escape into our world, but they can only do it by tracking down their doubles . . . and *replacing* them."

Jessica gasped. "What do you mean, *replacing*?"

"I mean that if Laura's doppelgänger was strong enough, she could have forced Laura into the doppelgänger dimension, and taken over her life. And since only the doppelgängers know how to go back and forth between our world and theirs, Laura could be trapped there forever."

Tears sprung to Jessica's eyes. "That could explain why Laura — or whoever it is — looked like she'd been in a fight. Do you really think she might have kidnapped our Laura — the good Laura?"

Robbie nodded gravely. "It happens a lot," he said. "In fact, there's a Web site —"

He was interrupted by the phone ringing.

Jessica hurried over to pick up the receiver.

"Jess, sweetie — is everything all right?"

Jessica recognized the voice on the other end of the line immediately. "Mom!" she said, relief flooding into her voice.

"I just had this terrible *feeling* that something was wrong," Mom continued. "Your dad says I'm being silly, but I just felt it in my bones."

"You're right this time, though, Mom," Jessica said urgently. "Something *is* wrong! Very wrong!"

Then the connection was cut.

"Mom?" Jessica said frantically. "Mom! Hello?"

But the phone in her hand was now just a useless piece of plastic, silent and dead. "The phone's stopped working!" she told Robbie.

The door opened just then. The babysitter stood in the doorway, holding Mom's big scissors from the kitchen drawer. She threw them on to a chair, points down, so they burst the cushion. "I can't stand the sound of phones ringing. These came in handy," she said.

Jessica saw from the look on Robbie's face that he was thinking the same thing as her: The babysitter must have used the scissors to cut the phone wire in the hall. And they didn't have cell phones. Mom wouldn't allow them to because she'd read about the health risks. Well, now their health really *was* at risk. They had no way of calling for help.

The babysitter walked across the room and slumped back in her chair in the shadows. Jessica and Robbie sat together on the sofa, completely still, not daring to move a muscle. The silence in the room somehow seemed louder than the computer game had been.

Now all Jessica could think about was whether Megan was OK. Without the phone or any way of communicating with the outside world, neither she nor Robbie could get help! She risked a sideways glance at her brother, knowing he'd be thinking the same thing. His face was arranged into a deep frown, as though he was listening intently for any sounds from their little sister.

Finally, Robbie spoke. "Can we go in the kitchen and make ourselves some food?" he asked, his voice trembling slightly.

Good one, Robbie! Jessica thought. *Please, please say yes, whoever you are, so we can just get out of this room and go upstairs and check that Megan's all right.*

"Do what you want," the babysitter said.

Jessica and Robbie breathed a joint sigh of relief and walked out of the room — not too fast, trying not to seem like they were in any sort of a hurry.

In the hall, Robbie nudged Jessica. "Put the kettle on," he whispered, "so she'll hear it boiling. But fill it right up to the top with water first, so it'll take a while to boil. Then we can go upstairs and check on Megan."

Jessica nodded and went into the kitchen. She took the kettle to the sink and let cold water gush in. When it was full, she put it on the stove and joined Robbie, who was standing in the doorway, gesturing at her to hurry.

"We could try to get out of the house," Robbie said, "and go next door for help."

"And leave Megan here? With *her*?" Jessica said.

"Of course not," Robbie replied. "But we can go up and get her, can't we? Then come down and take her with us?"

Jessica looked upstairs. It was totally silent.

"I hope she's all right," Jessica said anxiously.

They climbed the stairs, Robbie in front and Jessica following as fast as she could, trying to put her weight on the banister instead of her bad ankle. When they reached the top, Robbie switched on the light and they hurried across the landing.

The door to Megan's room was shut. The handle had been forcibly snapped off. The lock was jammed, making it impossible to open the door.

Jessica gasped. "Did Laura, or whoever she is, just snap off the handle with her bare hands?" she asked.

"Maybe," Robbie said. "Try putting your ear to the door and listening. Can you hear if Megan's all right in there?"

Jessica waited, but could hear nothing. She cupped her hands around her mouth and began to whisper as loudly as she dared, "Megan . . . Megan!" Part of her mind was crying out for her to hammer on the door, to break it down, just to see if Megan was all right. But the other half of her mind knew what would happen if she did — the babysitter would catch her and Robbie, and that would be worse than leaving Megan until they could get some help.

Still no reply. Megan's room was as silent as a tomb.

Robbie knocked gently on the door. "Megan?" he said, but there was no response. Jessica looked around desperately. There must be something — anything — they could do.

"Let's go to my room," Robbie said suddenly. "I'll show you something on the computer that might help us save Megan."

"What?" Jessica asked.

"A site I found that some kids started. There are

loads of stories about doppelgängers invading people's lives, and taking their places one by one."

"Are you sure it's not just some kind of a joke?" Jessica asked.

"Totally," Robbie confirmed. "The reports were deadly serious. The kids were scared out of their skulls."

"We can send out some e-mails, too," Jessica said as she followed Robbie to his room. "Maybe someone will come and help. There must be some way we could contact the police or something."

As Robbie turned on his bedroom light, the werewolf, vampire, and monster masks burst into view. But the only monster Jessica was concerned about right now was the one downstairs.

The computer screen on Robbie's desk was blank. "I'm sure I left it on," he said, walking over and moving the mouse back and forth.

"How long does it take to boot up?" Jessica asked, listening downstairs for any movement.

"Not long," Robbie replied. He pressed the switch, but nothing happened.

"Check the plug," Jessica said. "Maybe it's been pulled out of the wall."

Robbie crouched down by the side of the bed, pushing aside a pile of horror comics and a plastic bust of Frankenstein's monster. Then he gasped.

"What's the matter?" Jessica asked nervously.

"She's cut the wire," Robbie said. "Just like she did to the phone wire! She's cutting off all our means of communication. We have to get out of the house," he finished urgently.

"We're not leaving Megan here," Jessica said firmly.

There was a shout from the hallway. *"Where are you?"*

"W-we're coming," Jessica called back, trying her best not to stammer. She turned to Robbie. "Why do you think she's here? I mean . . . what do you think she wants?"

"Well, doppelgängers are the total opposite of their doubles," Robbie said slowly. "The good Laura loves boy-band music to death and the bad Laura finds it sickening. So . . ." He swallowed hard.

"What?" Jessica said.

"If the good Laura wanted to look after us and keep

us safe, then I guess the bad one . . . would want to hurt us."

"You two!" the babysitter yelled from downstairs. "Get down here now!"

"Just pretend everything's OK," Robbie whispered.

They made their way out of Robbie's room and down the stairs.

The babysitter was waiting for them at the bottom, looking very angry. She grabbed Robbie's arm. "Now it's *your* bedtime," she said. "So you can go straight back up again." And she began to march him up the stairs.

Jessica saw Robbie try to pull away — but it was clear that this Laura was far stronger than the real one. As they reached the landing, he threw a frightened glance at Jessica, his eyes pleading for help.

Jessica stood at the bottom of the stairs, desperately trying to figure out what to do. She knew she had to leave the house and raise the alarm before it was too late. But she also knew she'd never be able to get through the locks and chain on the front door before the babysitter caught her.

She ran to the back of the house.

The kitchen door was locked, and there was no sign of the key. The keys to the window locks had been removed, too.

She rushed out of the kitchen and into the living room. The same was true of the windows there. Jessica considered hammering on the glass, but she was sure that nobody would hear. If only it was one of those nights when the neighbors had a barbecue and there were lots of people in their backyard.

"Jessica!"

The babysitter stood in the doorway.

Jessica stared, frozen with fear, as the babysitter began to walk toward her.

And then there was a knock on the door.

"Wait here," the babysitter said curtly. She turned and left the living room, shutting the door behind her.

Jessica ran over to the door to listen. She heard the chain on the front door being removed, the two heavy locks being turned, and then the murmur of voices and footfalls on the stairs. Had her parents returned? Why had Laura unlocked the front door?

She opened the living room door as quietly as she

could and peeped out. The hallway was empty. And the chain and deadlock were off. Perhaps she really could get away!

Jessica limped down the hall as quickly as she could. Her twisted ankle shot flares of pain up her calf, but she didn't care. Anything was better than being captured by that thing.

As Jessica reached to pull the door open, another hand covered hers.

She turned to look up into the babysitter's glacial green eyes. Any lingering hope she had of leaving the house dissolved like steam.

"You don't think I would let you go out on your own, in the dark, at this time of night, do you?" the babysitter said with a darkly sinister smile. "You could get yourself into all kinds of danger. . . ."

Jessica realized that the babysitter had been tormenting her. Letting her think she might have a chance of escape — and then snatching it away.

"Time for bed . . ." the babysitter hissed. And she began to force Jessica slowly up the stairs.

Jessica wondered what the babysitter was going to do with her now. She wondered what had become of her brother and sister, and she felt tears stinging her eyes. She thought frantically for another way to escape. There was no way she'd be able to break free by force. She'd have to use trickery. Maybe if she pretended to go along with the babysitter, the babysitter would let down her guard and give Jessica a chance to think of something else. And then she had an idea. It was worth a try.

"There's no need to push me, Laura," Jessica said. "I'll go to bed willingly. I'm too tired to resist now. . . ."

"Good girl," the babysitter said, loosening her grip.

Jessica wrenched herself free and shot up the rest of the stairs toward her room. She felt no pain in her ankle — it was as if it had gone numb with fear, like the rest of her. At the landing she looked back to see the babysitter giving chase, a furious snarl on her face.

Jessica flung herself into her room and dashed over to her CD player.

Yes!

It *was* just as she'd remembered. The CD cover to her favorite boy band's latest album was on top of the player. That meant the CD was still inside.

She pressed PLAY and heard the CD begin to whirr into place.

Hurry, hurry, she thought, switching the volume up high.

The babysitter entered the room and closed the bedroom door, her face white with fury. As she walked toward Jessica, music began to flood out of the speakers.

The babysitter stopped still, clutching her ears. She shook her head viciously from side to side, before finally tearing herself out of the room and hurrying back down the stairs.

Jessica felt sick with relief. She turned the music up as loud as it would go — louder than she'd ever dared play it before. The lampshade hanging from the ceiling began to shake and the furniture in her bedroom rattled like castanets.

Soon, she thought, *the neighbors will complain. They'll call the police . . . or come around knocking themselves. Then we'll be OK.*

Then suddenly, the music stopped and the whole house was swallowed by darkness.

Jessica had a nightmare thought: There was a switch

just inside the pantry that turned off all the electricity in the house; the babysitter must have flicked that switch.

Jessica limped out to the landing and looked over the rail.

The babysitter was now standing in the gloom at the foot of the stairs.

"Why are you doing this? Get out of our house!" Jessica screamed at her.

The babysitter began to climb. Step by slow step, coming up the stairs to get her.

A shaft of light from a streetlight shone in through the landing window. The babysitter's shadow rose slowly up the wall, growing nearer and nearer.

Jessica stumbled back into her bedroom. *It really is the end this time,* she thought.

The babysitter appeared in the doorway and Jessica wanted to scream, but her throat was frozen with terror.

Then she heard a rattling noise downstairs. Somebody was at the front door. Could it be. . . ?

"Laura? Why are the lights off? Did the fuse blow?"

Yes! Her parents were back!

The babysitter stood still, clearly deciding how to deal with this unexpected development.

And then the lights burst back into full brightness. Her parents had switched the electricity back on. Jessica's music came on again, and the babysitter rushed out of her room and back down the stairs.

Her heart still racing, Jessica turned the music down. She wanted to shout to Dad, but she was breathless with relief. She could barely manage a whisper; she could barely move.

She heard talking down there and listened hard.

"Sorry about that. I was just looking for the fuse box myself," the babysitter said.

"Don't worry. And sorry I was so snappy earlier," Jessica heard Dad reply.

"That's all right," the babysitter said, "but I can hardly stay awake, I'm so tired. Would you mind giving me a lift home?"

"Not at all," Dad replied.

"I'll come, too," said Mom. "You can show me what you've done with your apartment. You told me about it last week. It's only just around the corner, isn't it? Then we'll get right back for the kids."

"No! Don't go with her!" Jessica shouted. But the words came out as a hoarse croak.

Desperately, she limped back out to the landing, her eyes leaking tears and her ankle throbbing. She caught her reflection in the landing mirror as she passed. Her face was as white as a corpse. She looked like Robbie had been practicing his makeup skills on her.

But she was too late. The front door had shut behind them.

She hobbled down the stairs as fast as she could and threw open the front door. But the family car had already moved off down the drive with that — *monster* — inside and was accelerating down the road.

Jessica wondered if she'd ever see her parents again. And then everything went black.

When Jessica came to, the front door was opening. With a gasp, she tried to fling herself back up the stairs, but the pain in her ankle stabbed at her and she stayed sprawled out on the floor. A scream built up in her throat. She was about to let it out, when she saw . . .

Dad, standing in the doorway, smiling, and making way for Mom to pass by him. They were back from taking the babysitter home. And they both looked OK.

"What are you doing down there?" Dad asked. "You should be in bed."

Jessica had so much to explain to them. "Dad, I don't know where to begin. But you have to call the police," she stammered.

"The police?" Dad said, looking concerned. "Here." He held out a hand to pull her up.

Jessica reached out to take it, and then she pulled away uneasily. It was his left hand.

She cast her gaze from Dad's face to Mom's face, from Dad's newly green eyes to Mom's newly green eyes.

Reeling with horror, Jessica got her good leg under her, pushed herself up, and began to back away up the stairs.

"Jess, what is it?" Dad said, coming after her. His voice sounded a little unusual.

As though he had a cold. Just like Laura's had sounded.

"Keep away from me," Jessica said. "I know what you are."

"What we are? Jessica — did you have a nightmare?" Dad reached out for her again.

Jessica pulled away. "You want to replace me with my evil double," she stammered.

She turned and began to hobble upstairs away from them both — and then stopped as she caught sight of two figures standing at the top, looking back down at her.

She swayed for a second on her good leg, and then called out to them. "Robbie? Megan? Are you all right?"

"We're fine, Jess," Robbie replied, taking Megan's hand. "And now you can be, too."

Jessica's brother and sister stepped into the light.

Their green eyes glinted as they made their way down the stairs toward her.

Jessica knew she wouldn't be able to fight her parents' doppelgängers — they were too strong. But her siblings' evil doubles were smaller.

Ignoring the pain in her ankle, Jessica rushed up the stairs as fast as she could, charging toward Robbie and Megan. They toppled to the ground as Jessica stormed past, racing toward her bedroom. She threw herself inside and slammed the door.

"That wasn't very nice!" the evil Robbie cried, pounding on the door.

"Come out, Jessica," the other doppelgänger said, in Megan's sweet voice, "I just want to play."

Jessica's heart broke just then. But she couldn't let herself think about what had happened to her brother and sister, or the fear and misery would overwhelm her. She needed a plan.

She flipped the lock on the door, knowing it wouldn't keep the doubles out for long. *Think, think!* she ordered herself as the panic flooded her brain. She could barely breathe.

Her eyes darted around the room, searching for something, *anything* that could help — maybe a weapon, maybe an escape. . . .

Just outside her bedroom window was a tall oak tree with wobbly branches that stretched toward the house. Jessica had always wondered whether she would be able to reach it from her window. Now was the time to find out.

She crept toward the window and slipped it open, hoping the doppelgängers wouldn't realize what she was doing.

"Young lady, you come out here this instant!" her father's voice demanded.

"We have a treat for you," her mother added, with an evil cackle.

Jessica shuddered, and climbed up onto the window frame. There were a few feet of space between her and the branch — and it was a *long* way down.

"If you won't come out," her father warned, "we're coming in."

Jessica held her breath, and for a moment, there was dead silence. Then a sharp, angry sound of cracking wood. Jessica's heart seized. She remembered: the small axe down in the basement, next to her father's tools. It looked like the doppelgänger knew about it, too.

"Ready or not," Megan announced, with a creepy, high-pitched giggle. "Here we —"

Jessica took a deep breath — and launched herself into the air. For a moment, it felt like she was floating.

And then the moment stretched too long, and she knew she'd missed the branch.

I'm going to fall, she thought miserably. *I'm going to crash into the ground and —*

Her fingers wrapped around the knobby branch, and she dangled in mid-air, her arm nearly wrenched out of its socket. But she held on, and pulled herself up into the tree. And as the evil doubles watched helplessly from her window, she scrambled down the trunk and ran away as fast as she could, disappearing into the darkness.

Jessica hid in the park, crouched in a small grove of trees on the south end. She waited there for hours, shivering and crying, wondering what had happened to her family — her *real* family. Would she ever see them again?

The police would never believe her — no grown-up would. They would just send her back to her "parents," and that would be the end of her.

No, she was on her own now.

She would have to watch her new family carefully — and wait. Somehow, she might find a way to defeat them. Her *true* family was trapped in some horrible, far-off place, surrounded by unspeakable evil. She was their only hope, and she refused to let them down.

I'll do whatever it takes, she silently promised each of them. *I* will *get you back*.

Someday.

Don't escape yet! Here's an exclusive sneak peek from "Is Anybody There?" — just one of three terrifying tales to be found in

THE MIDNIGHT LIBRARY

END GAME

Posters of the missing boy hung in a row at the back of the stage. Luke Benton was pleasant-looking, blond, with a scattering of freckles. He wore a slightly bashful smile as if he couldn't quite believe he was being photographed. The picture that had been used for the posters was Luke's last school photo, taken the day he vanished. He had been wearing his school blazer and tie, and, though you couldn't see them in the picture, new black sneakers with a silver trim. His entire outfit had been immortalized by "the last seen wearing" description on all the "Missing" posters that had been plastered around town.

Someone opened the door to the hall and the posters rustled in the breeze. Juliet Somerville made a mental note to tape them down at all four corners after the rehearsal. Luke's memorial service was going to be in two days' time, and if the posters were waving around at the back of the stage, that would be a distraction to everyone in the hall.

Juliet figured it would be quicker to do it herself than to mention it to Miss Worth. Their principal could take the simplest idea and over-complicate it. She had already turned the rehearsal for the memorial service into a three-ringed circus.

Privately, Juliet found it tasteless. Luke hadn't been seen for over a year. His phone hadn't been used, and no money had been taken out of his bank account. He had to be gone forever. He should be remembered in a church service or something, not a performance where people got stage fright and fretted about how they would look under the lights.

Miss Worth clapped her hands above the chatter in the hall until she had everyone's attention. "Now, light desk — *light desk!* — thank you . . . and sound desk . . .

both ready? Good. Now, can everyone who is going to read a tribute to Luke form a line on the left side of the stage . . . no, the *left* side . . . in alphabetical order of first name . . . or should that be order of age? Hmmm . . ."

Juliet nudged her best friend Christine. "How about order of shoe size?" she whispered.

But Christine wasn't in a mood for jokes. "Julie, I think Mark just looked at me!" she hissed. She stared across the hall. "Look! He just did it again!"

Juliet followed her gaze, trying not to let her doubt show on her face. Mark Logan and his best friend Daniel Gardner were sitting together at the back of the hall. Mark had a stocky, powerful frame; Daniel was taller and darker, with really floppy bangs. Like most of the boys, they were in their football uniforms. All of Luke's teammates were going to wear their gear for the service as part of their tribute. If Mark had been looking at Christine, he wasn't now. He and Dan had their heads bowed together, deep in some private conversation.

"I wonder what they're talking about," Christine whispered. "I bet it's about Luke. Mark is such a deep thinker. He's so intellectual. He'll be sharing his thoughts about how loss and bereavement should make us appreciate the finer things of life — and draw us closer together in love."

Juliet shot her friend a quick glance to check if she was being serious. Unfortunately, she was. "Oh, definitely," she agreed. "Or maybe he scored a really cool touchdown one time and he's telling Daniel all about it."

Christine scowled. "You are such a cynic! They were Luke's closest friends, you know that."

"So why didn't they volunteer to read tributes?" Juliet asked.

"Oh, Julie, you don't measure friendship like that! Think about it. I mean, losing your best friend overnight — never even finding a clue, just *losing* him — what must that be like? Of course they don't want to stand up in front of everyone. They probably haven't even begun to deal with what happened to Luke."

"They could have gotten help, I don't know, some sort of counseling," Juliet pointed out. She wasn't sure why; perhaps she just wanted to be stubborn — and wanted to puncture Christine's inflated view of Mark. In the weeks after the disappearance, the school had been overrun with well-meaning professionals urging Luke's fellow students to put their emotions into words.

"And why should they? Why should they talk to some stranger about their inner feelings?" Christine's voice grew warm. "They need someone who knows them, knows exactly what they're going through."

In other words, Juliet thought, *they should talk to you!* But she didn't say it out loud. It would be mean — and maybe Christine could help the boys after all. As the first anniversary of Luke's disappearance drew nearer, Mark and Daniel had become more and more withdrawn. If anyone approached them, even just brushed against them in the hallway, they could be snappish and irritable. So if Christine was able to help — well, good for her. She certainly couldn't do any harm.

Juliet looked down at the piece of paper in her hands. She had finished writing her tribute after a lot of crossing out and revision. *I first met Luke on our first day at this school, four years ago —*

Tears stung her eyes, and she folded the paper up again. She would have to practice a lot more before she could stand up in front of everyone without losing it. . . .

What really happened to Luke? Find out soon!

SKULL'S OUT!
Available in November 2006

3 TERRIFYING TALES FROM
THE MIDNIGHT LIBRARY
END GAME
DAMIEN GRAVES
SCHOLASTIC